Life Skills for Young Adults:
How to Manage Money, Find a Job, Stay Fit, Eat Healthy and Live Independently

Everything a Teen Should Know Before Leaving Home

Ferne Bowe

Life Skills for Young Adults: How to Manage Money, Find a Job, Stay Fit, Eat Healthy and Live Independently. Everything a Teen Should Know Before Leaving Home (suitable for college & high school students)

Copyright © 2022 Ferne Bowe

Published by: Bemberton Ltd

All rights reserved. No part of this book or any portion thereof may be reproduced in any form by any electronic or mechanical means, without permission in writing from the publisher, except for the use of brief quotes in a book review.

The publisher accepts no legal responsibility for any action taken by the reader, including but not limited to financial losses or damages, both directly or indirectly, incurred as a result of the content in this book.

ISBN: 978-1-7396378-4-2

Disclaimer: The information in this book is general and designed to be for information only. While every effort has been made to ensure it is wholly accurate and complete, it is for general information only. It is not intended, nor should it be taken as professional advice. The author gives no warranties or undertakings whatsoever concerning the content. For matters of a medical nature, the reader should consult a doctor or other healthcare professional for specific health-related advice. In addition, the reader should consult with a professional financial advisor before making any significant decisions regarding finances or money matters.

The reader accepts that the author is not responsible for any action, including but not limited to losses, both directly or indirectly, incurred by the reader as a result of the content in this book.

SOMETHING FOR YOU!

Get your FREE Life Skills Printable Templates

SCAN QR CODE TO
GET YOUR COPY

CONTENTS

7   Introduction

9   **Chapter 1.** Managing Your Money & Budgeting

27 **Chapter 2.** The Basics of Saving & Investing

37 **Chapter 3.** A Simple Guide to Renting

41 **Chapter 4.** Cooking & Food Skills

63 **Chapter 5.** Living a Healthy Lifestyle & Caring for Your Mental Health

79 **Chapter 6.** Personal Healthcare & Basic First Aid

93 **Chapter 7.** Maintaining Relationships: Social Skills, Networking, and Communication

105 **Chapter 8.** How to Manage a Home

121 **Chapter 9.** Organization & Time Management

133 **Chapter 10.** Solving Problems & Decision-Making Skills

141 **Chapter 11.** Kickstarting Your Career

INTRODUCTION

Congratulations, you're a young adult! You've made it, and now you're about to embark on the next phase of your life. You're about to become independent and leave the nest. But before you do, there are some things you need to know. Things that they don't teach you in high school. Things that will help you succeed in the real world.

We're talking about life skills.

We all know that life skills are important, but what exactly are they? **Life skills are the abilities and knowledge that we need to help us navigate through everyday life.** They include everything from time management and decision making to communication and relationship building. They are all the practical skills, such as cooking and budgeting, that we need to function independently.

So why are life skills so critical? Because they give us the ability to tackle anything that comes our way. They prepare us for the challenges of adulthood and help us to become well-rounded, successful individuals.

Think about it this way, would you rather be stranded on a deserted island with someone who knows how to build a shelter and start a fire or someone who can recite all the state capitals? We all know the answer to that.

Learning life skills is essential for every young adult. But unfortunately, many of these skills are not taught in school. They are learned outside of the classroom through experience and trial and error. You won't sit an exam on how to rent your first apartment or save smart, but these are all essential life skills you need to know.

That's what this book is for. It's a practical guide that will give you the tools you need to succeed in the real world. And while it's designed to be read cover to cover, you can also dip in and out of it as you need to. So, if you're looking for advice on managing your finances, you can head straight to that chapter. Or, if you need some tips on relationships, then that's where you'll find them. Furthermore, you'll find key information highlighted in bold throughout the book so that you can quickly scan and find what you're looking for.

So, what are you waiting for? It's time to learn the life skills to help you thrive in the real world!

Chapter 1

MANAGING YOUR MONEY & BUDGETING

Leaving home and heading out into the big wide world is an exciting time—but it can also be daunting, especially when it comes to money and budgeting. It's essential to learn the skills outlined in this chapter before you leave home to handle your finances responsibly and avoid any potential problems down the road.

This chapter will discuss some essential money and budgeting skills that every young adult should learn. We'll cover everything from creating a budget to managing your expenses wisely. So whether you're just starting out in college or about to graduate, read on for some essential tips!

Please note that information in this chapter is for information only and should not be taken as professional financial advice. You should consult with a financial advisor before making any significant decisions regarding your finances.

What Is Budgeting & Why Is It Important?

Learning how to budget is the most critical money management skill. A budget allows you to track your expenses and ensure that you're not spending more than you can afford. It also helps you plan for the future and save for important goals like a car or a down payment on a house.

How to Create a Budget

There is no one "right" way to create a budget—it depends on your individual needs and circumstances. But here are some tips on how to get started:

- **Start by calculating your monthly expenses.** This includes all your outgoings, from your rent to your grocery bill. Write these down in a budget worksheet or on a piece of paper. You may find it helpful to split these into two categories. Fixed expenses, such as rent or car payments, don't change month-to-month. Variable expenses, like groceries or entertainment, vary from month to month. You might find it helpful to break these into necessities & wants. Necessities are things like food, shelter, and clothing—while wants are things like cable TV or that new party outfit.

- **Next, calculate your income.** This is the total amount of money you bring in each month and includes all of the money you earn from wages, investments, and other sources of income. Say you make $200 waiting tables at the weekend, and your allowance is $300. Your total monthly income would be $500.

▶ **Now it's time to create your budget!** Look at your expenses and see what you can afford to spend each month. If your total monthly costs are more than your total monthly income, you'll need to make some adjustments. You may need to cut back on some of your wants or find a way to increase your income. On the other hand, if your total monthly expenses are less than your total monthly income, you can use the extra money to save or invest.

▶ **Make sure you have some "emergency" funds to fall back on.** This is your insurance and will cover unexpected expenses if your budget falls short or your circumstances unexpectedly change.

▶ **Be patient!** It may take a little time to tweak your budget and make it work. But with a bit of effort, you'll be able to manage your finances successfully.

▶ Finally, be sure to **revise your budget regularly** as your income and expenses change.

How to Choose a Bank and Open a Bank Account

To budget effectively, you need to choose and open a bank account. This is a crucial way to manage your money and take charge of your financial responsibilities.

First, you must choose the bank and account that suits you best.

There are many different financial institutions and bank accounts out there, so it's worth shopping around as many offer incentives to new customers. Some accounts charge a monthly fee if you don't bring in a certain amount each month. Still, there are perks attached to these accounts like higher interest rates, free overdrafts, discounts, gifts, or free insurance. At the same time, others offer online customer service only, which may not suit everyone.

Before deciding, determine what is important to you, then research and compare what's on offer.

> **To open your account, you usually have to:**
> - Apply using an application form on the bank's website
> - Pass the identity and security checks (sometimes this means visiting the bank, while some will complete online security checks)
> - Put some money into your account to activate it.

Each month, you should receive a statement from your bank. Most banks give you the option to receive online statements or a paper statement by mail.

How to Read a Bank Statement

It's a good habit to check your bank statement regularly to keep on top of your expenses and to ensure you are not subject to fraud. You can usually check your transactions via mobile banking apps or online accounts.

Managing Your Money & Budgeting

When checking your statement, you should:
- Review all transactions to ensure that they are correct and legitimate.
- Look for any suspicious charges or sudden increases in your transaction history. Check that you recognize each transaction.
- Report any unusual activity immediately to your bank so that they can investigate the issue and help protect you from fraud.
- Make a note of regular payments, direct debits, or bills to budget wisely.
- Cancel unnecessary monthly payments. Simply log into your online account to view, edit or cancel.

Know Your Payments — Direct Debits, Standing Orders, and Recurring Payments

Direct debits and standing orders are regular payments on your bank account that come out regularly (usually on a specific date) every month.

Standing orders are set up by you, and you can change them or cancel them at any time. An example might be your monthly rent.

Direct debits are set up by the company you're paying and are pulled from your bank account (for example, your utility bill or gym membership). They can only be changed or canceled with the company's permission.

Recurring payments are set up on your debit or credit card and charged on a pre-arranged payment schedule. The money is charged to your card on the agreed date. An example of a recurring payment would be if you subscribed to a monthly streaming service, and they charged your card on the same date each month.

How to Manage Your Money Wisely

Once you have a budget in place, it's essential to follow it closely. This means making sure that you don't spend more than you can afford each month and saving for the future.

Here are a few tips on how to manage your money wisely:

- **Avoid impulse buying.** If you see something you want, wait a few days before deciding whether or not to buy it. This will give you time to think about whether or not you need it.

- **Create a savings goal.** It's helpful to have a savings account for emergencies. Still, it's also good to save for specific items like a car or a down payment on a house. No matter how low your income, aim to save 20% of your income each month. Pay yourself first—before you pay any of your other bills, make sure you put money into your savings account.

- **Use cash instead of credit cards.** Credit cards can be tempting, especially when you're short on money. But they can also lead to debt if you're not careful. Use cash whenever possible to track precisely how much money you're spending.

- **Use a debit card instead of a credit card.** When you use a debit card, you're spending the money you already have. Whereas when you use a credit card, you're borrowing money that you may not be able to pay back. This helps you stay within your budget, and it also helps you avoid getting into debt.

- **Delete shopping apps from your phone.** If you have a hard time resisting the temptation to buy things, delete shopping apps from your phone. This will help you to avoid temptation.

- **Eat in instead of eating out.** Eating out can be expensive, especially if you're doing it often. Try to cook at home as much as possible to save money.

- **Look for discounts and deals.** There are plenty of ways to save money on everyday items. Look for bargains at stores, coupons online, and sales at your favorite retailers. Many stores offer discounts for students, so be sure to take advantage of them.

- **Buy used.** One way to save money on big-ticket items is to buy them used. You can find used cars, furniture, and even clothes at garage sales, consignment shops, and online marketplaces like eBay or Craigslist.

- **Skip the upgrade.** Do you really need the new phone with the better camera? Make do with what you have until you can afford to upgrade. This goes for other big-ticket items as well. If you don't need the newest model, save your money and buy the older one.

- **Cancel recurring monthly subscription services.** Many of these services offer free trials and then automatically revert to a monthly or annual recurring subscription. Check your bank statements, and cancel those you don't use or need.

- **Deal with financial stress head-on.** If you're feeling overwhelmed by your finances, don't try to ignore the problem. Deal with it head-on and come up with a plan to fix it.

How to Make Money

There are plenty of ways to make extra money if you need it. Here are a few ideas:

- **Start a side hustle.** A side hustle is a job or project you do in your spare time. It can be anything from freelance writing to dog walking.

- **Sell unwanted items online.** If you have any extra clothes, furniture, or other items lying around, sell them online to make some extra cash.

- **Get a weekend job.** If you need more money quickly, consider getting a weekend job. This can be anything from working in a restaurant to driving for Uber.

- **Rent out a room in your house.** If you have an extra room in your house, rent it out to make some extra cash. This can be a great way to cover your expenses, especially if you're unsure what you want to do after college.

- **Invest in stocks or mutual funds.** Consider investing in stocks or mutual funds if you have some money to spare. This can be a great way to make money over time, and it's a relatively low-risk investment.

- **Start a blog or online business.** If you're interested in starting your own business, consider creating a blog or starting an online business. This can be a great way to make money while working from home.

- **Become a tutor.** If you're good at a particular subject, consider becoming a tutor. You can offer your services online or in person.

- **Participate in online surveys.** Many websites pay you for completing online surveys. This is a great way to make extra money without leaving your house.

- **Start a savings challenge.** A savings challenge is a great way to motivate yourself to save money. Choose a goal, like saving 20% of your income each month or saving $1,000 in six months, and then work towards it.

Managing your money can seem like a daunting task, but if you take it one step at a time, you'll be able to manage your finances successfully.

Borrowing: Debt, Credit Cards, and Mortgages

There may be times when your monthly income doesn't cover your expenses, and you need to borrow money to make ends meet. Or you may want to buy a new car or home, and you need to finance the purchase with a loan.

Borrowing, debt, and loans are perfectly normal and common. Most people have some form of debt (e.g., a mortgage, student loan, credit card debt). The key is to understand the implications of borrowing money and managing your debt responsibly to avoid becoming a burden.

What Are Credit Cards?

Credit cards can be handy if used wisely. They can help you build your credit rating. Sometimes they provide a period of interest-free credit which can be helpful if you want to buy something urgently but don't have enough money in the bank.

However, they are an expensive method of borrowing unless you pay back the total balance every month.

What Is APR?

The interest you pay on a credit card is called APR. Let's explore what that means.

APR stands for **Annual Percentage Rate**. It is the interest rate charged on a loan, credit card, or other borrowing product. The APR is the cost of borrowing money, expressed as a percentage of the amount you borrow. For example, if you're charged an APR of 12%, it costs you $12 to borrow $100 for one year.

Remember, APR only covers interest, so any further fees or fines are not included in this. On certain products, APR can be extremely high. For example, the APR on some credit cards can be over 30%. This is why it's important to understand what you're being charged and to keep up with your monthly payments.

Many people prefer to use an overdraft or a bank loan as they are less expensive for longer-term borrowing.

Overdrafts and Loans

An overdraft is a loan from your bank that lets you spend more money than you have in your account. Most banks will allow you to do this, but you have to agree to the amount before going overdrawn. They may also charge you fees and interest on your overdrawn amount. Many people use overdrafts as an emergency fund to tide themselves over until they get paid.

A loan is when you borrow money from a lender and agree to pay it back over a period of time. The borrower pays interest on the loan, and this is added to the amount you need to repay. The borrower pays a fixed amount each week or month until the loan is fully repaid.

Buying a House: How Do Mortgages Work?

Buying a home can give you security and a place to call your own. But it's not always easy to get on the property ladder and is a big financial commitment. Though you may not be quite ready to take that step now, it helps to understand how mortgages work so you can make an informed decision when the time comes.

A mortgage is a loan that you take out to buy a property. The property is used as collateral, which means that if you can't repay the loan, the lender can repossess the property and sell it to recoup their money. There are two different types of mortgage—interest only and repayment.

Interest-only mortgages

With an interest-only mortgage, when you pay your mortgage each month, you are only paying the interest and nothing off your mortgage balance. This means that your debt will not reduce, and you'll still owe the full balance of your mortgage at the end of your mortgage term.

Repayment mortgages

With a repayment mortgage when you make monthly repayments, you cover the interest and a contribution towards your mortgage balance too. This means your debt will reduce, and at the end of the term, your balance will be paid, and you will own your property outright. Repayment mortgages are usually repaid over 25 years, but this can depend on the lender.

How Much Can I Borrow?

The amount you can borrow will depend on your monthly income, monthly expenses, employment status, and credit history.

Most lenders apply a debt to income ratio. They want you to be able to cover your mortgage payments each month comfortably, so they don't want you to spend more than 31–36% of your monthly income on your housing debts. This includes not just the repayment of the mortgage but also insurance and taxes.

For example:
If you earn $3,500 per month, the maximum amount you can afford to spend on your mortgage is $1,085-$1,260

You can reduce your monthly mortgage payments if you can put down a larger down payment. The down payment is the amount you pay upfront when you purchase the property.

For example:
If you're buying a $200,000 house and have a 20% down payment of $40,000, your monthly payments will be lower than if you had a 10% down payment of $20,000.

This is because you're borrowing less money and therefore pay less interest each month.

You can use a mortgage calculator to determine how much you could afford to borrow and what your monthly payments would be.

Credit Profile

Your credit score is a calculation that represents your creditworthiness. Lenders use it to decide whether or not to give you a loan and at what interest rate.

Your credit score is based on your credit history, which is a record of your past activity, including the types of credit you already have and your repayment behavior.

The better your credit history, the higher your credit score will be, and the more likely you will be approved for a loan at a favorable interest rate.

It's a good idea to check your credit report regularly to ensure that the information collated is correct. You can do this via one of the leading online credit reporting agencies for free.

What Affects Your Credit Profile?

There are several factors that can affect your credit score, including:

- **New credit applications.** Applying for multiple credit products simultaneously can negatively impact your credit score.

- **The mix of credit products.** A good blend of well-maintained products (e.g. credit cards, loans, etc.) can improve your score.

- **Your payment history** and whether you have been paying your bills on time.

▶ **Your total debt.** Too much debt will impact the amount you can borrow.

▶ **Your credit history age.** The older your credit history, the better your credit score will be.

TOP TIPS: Improve Your Credit Score

▶ Make all regular payments on time. This shows lenders you are reliable and responsible.

▶ Check your credit report for errors and report any you find

▶ Don't use too much credit. Stay well below your limit — use about 30% of your credit and if you are able to, try to keep old accounts open. This demonstrates a long, well-managed credit history.

Borrowing money is a part of life for most people, but by keeping on top of your repayments and understanding the ins and outs of borrowing, you can ensure it doesn't become a burden.

How to Avoid Fraud and Scams

With the rise of online shopping, social media, and online banking, there has also been a rise in fraud and identity theft.

Fraudsters are opportunists and will target anyone they think they can easily scam. They often create fake websites, phone numbers, or social media profiles to trick people into giving them personal information and money. It's helpful to be aware of the different types of scams to protect yourself from them.

> **Some common types of fraud include:**
> - **Phishing** is where fraudsters pose as a trusted person or organization to trick you into revealing personal information or login details. They typically do this by sending a text, instant message, or email.
> - **Vishing** is where fraudsters use automated voice messages or calls posing as a legitimate company. The aim is to collect your personal information, such as credit card details, PIN, or any digital passcodes or passwords.
> - **Social engineering** is where fraudsters deceive people into disclosing confidential or personal information. This is also known as psychological manipulation.
> - **Online scams** are becoming more and more common and take many forms. They can occur through emails, websites, social media, and even over the phone, when fake goods or trials may be offered. For example, some scams involve copycat official websites, where the fraudsters create a website that looks very similar to a legitimate one. Other scams involve fake prize draws, holiday accommodation, and even online dating. The fraudster's goal is always the same: to trick people into sharing personal information, login details, or financial data.

Although there are many scams out there, don't worry; there are some simple steps that you can take to reduce your risk.

Managing Your Money & Budgeting

Online Safety Tips

Never share passwords

Never share your passwords or PIN with others, especially via text, email, cell or in person

Use strong passwords

including symbols, numbers, capital letters and never reuse passwords across different sites.

Listen to your gut

If it doesn't feel right or it sounds too good to be true, don't go through with it - hang up, or don't click the link, and report the email. You should also contact your bank too!

Stop and think

Before clicking on any links in an email, text, or message. Always check the domain name & the email address matches the name of the person or business.

Limit your info

Limit the personal information you display on your public social media accounts. This includes your address, date of birth and age etc.

Turn on 2FA

Where possible, turn on two-factor authentication. Consider using a password manager tool, such as LastPass.

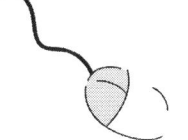

Stay safe online!

Now that we've covered managing your money, it's time to take it that step further in chapter 2 by discussing the basics around saving and investing!

Chapter 2

THE BASICS OF SAVING & INVESTING

What's the one thing you've always dreamed of buying but haven't had the money to purchase? A car? A new bike? A trip abroad?

Saving and investing for the future is one of the most important things you can do for yourself. By setting aside money when you're young, you'll have time to let your money grow over time. And if you continue to save consistently, you can achieve your financial goals and make your dreams a reality.

Please note that information in this chapter is for information only and should not be taken or construed as financial advice. While every effort is made to ensure the information is accurate it is no substitute for professional advice. You should consult with a financial advisor before making any significant decisions regarding your finances.

How to Save Smart to Get Ahead

When you save money, you're essentially putting it aside to use in the future. You can save for various purposes, such as retirement, a rainy-day fund, or a down payment on a house. While saving may sound boring, it's one of the smartest things you can do. It's your path to financial independence.

Saving is an accomplishment, and it's something to be proud of. You have the satisfaction of knowing that you're doing something responsible for your future, but you can also enjoy the peace of mind that comes with knowing you have money saved up in case of an emergency.

There are a few different ways to save money.

Many banks offer **instant access savings accounts** that allow you to earn interest on your deposited money without access restrictions. The rate of interest you make will depend on the type of account and the bank where you invest your money. Typically, you'll earn around 2% interest for an instant access savings account.

Meaning if you invest $100 and the interest is 2% at the end of the year, your investment will be worth $102.

This is a great low-risk investment option if you don't want to tie up your money for an extended period.

TOP TIP: Automate Your Savings

One of the smartest ways to save is to set up a system where a certain amount of money is transferred from your checking account to your savings account automatically each month. This can be a great way to make sure you're always saving for the future without thinking about it.

Depending on your goals, you may also want to consider investing.

How Investing Works

Investing is essentially putting your money into something with the expectation of earning a return. It's a way to grow your money over time, and it can be a great way to reach your financial goals.

When you invest, you're buying assets such as stocks, bonds, or real estate. These assets usually offer higher returns than savings accounts but have higher risk levels. This means there is a risk that your investments could lose money if the market takes a downturn.

Before deciding if investing is right for you, you should **consider your goals, financial situation, and risk tolerance.**

You should set yourself a limit—don't invest all of your money and be sure to consider your investments carefully. Many people find it helpful to seek advice from a financial advisor or an investment expert.

If you're saving for a holiday, a car, or a new gadget, a savings account could be a better option than investing. On the other hand, if you're comfortable taking on more risk and have a longer time horizon, you may want to consider investing in stocks or mutual funds.

Stocks and fund assets often offer higher returns but come with more risk. The key is to remain invested, even when the market drops. The longer you're willing to invest, the more likely you will see positive returns. And if you start early, you'll have plenty of time to let your money grow via the magic of compounding.

The Wonders of Compound Interest

Compounding is one of the most powerful tools you have to save money. This is because compound interest allows your money to grow exponentially over time.

Your **interest is added to your initial investment when you earn through compounding,** so both the initial sum and the interest make interest.

Let's take a look at an example:
Assume you invest $1,000 in a savings account that pays 5% compound interest. At the end of the first year, your investment will be worth $1,050.

In the second year, you earn the 5% interest on $1050, so at the end of that year, your investment will be worth $1,102.50.

And at the end of the third year, your investment will be worth $1,157.63.

As you can see, your investment grows at a much faster rate.

The key is to start saving at a young age, so you have longer to enjoy the benefits of compound interest.

Life Skills for Young Adults

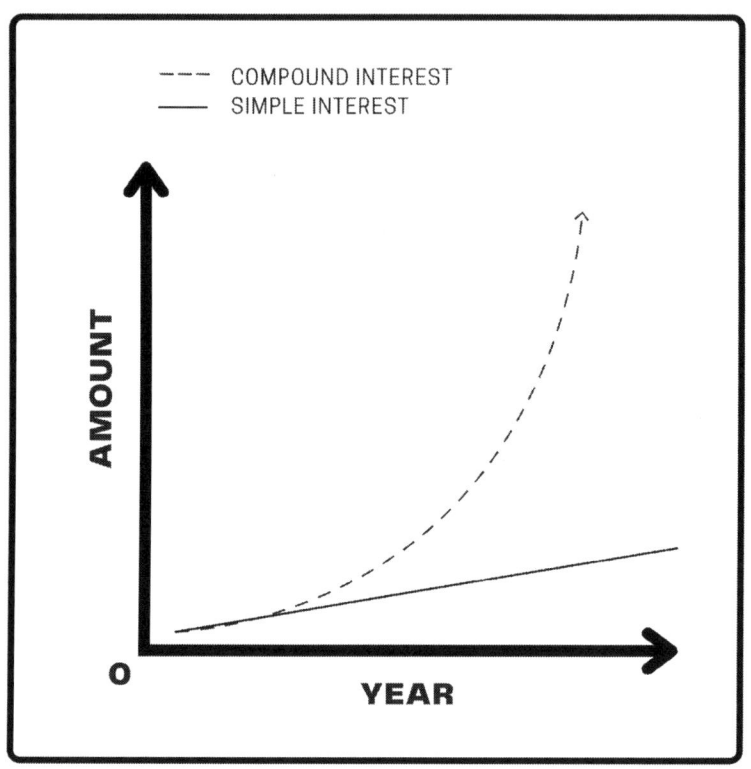

Let's take a look at another example:

Imagine 20-year-old Jon invests $1,000 today and leaves it untouched until he retires at 70. If he earns 7% interest every year, Jon's $1,000 will have turned into $29,457 by the time he's 70.

But let's say Annie waited until she was 30 before she invested $1,000. Even if she earned the same 7% interest, her investment would only grow to $14,974 by the time she retires at 70.

The longer you wait to start investing, the more difficult it becomes to catch up.

If you don't have a large lump sum to put away now, **small monthly contributions make a massive difference in the long run.** Even if you can't afford to invest a lot of money each month, your contributions will still add up.

For example, if Jon invests $20 per month until he's 70, he'll have invested $12,000. But his investment will be worth more than $100,000 thanks to compound interest (on a 7% interest rate).

That's the power of starting early and letting your money grow over time!

That's the power of compound interest!

How to Invest in Stocks and Shares

You're never too young to start investing. In fact, one of the best things about stocks is that you don't need a lot of money to get started. But it's important to understand the risks involved before you begin investing.

When you buy a stock (or share), you're buying a piece of a company. For example, if you own Apple stock, you own a small part of the company. **The price of a stock goes up and down** depending on how well the company is doing. If the company does well, the stock price will go up. If the company does poorly, the stock price will go down. This means that **there is a risk that you could lose money if you invest in stocks.**

There are a few different ways to invest in stocks. You can buy shares in individual companies or invest in mutual funds or exchange-traded funds (ETFs).

A mutual fund is a collection of stocks from different companies, while an ETF tracks an index, such as the S&P 500, a collection of 500 of the largest US companies.

When you invest in a mutual fund or ETF, you're spreading your risk across many companies. This means that if one company performs poorly in the index, it won't impact your overall investment as much.

When it comes to stocks and shares, it's important to remember that there's no such thing as a guaranteed return. The key is your time horizon: the longer you're willing to wait, the more likely you are to see a positive return.

> **How to start investing:**
> If you're ready to start investing, there are a few things you need to do first.
> 1. **Figure out how much money you can afford to invest.** Remembering investing is a long-term game, so you should be comfortable locking your money away for at least five years. There's a saying that you should only invest what you can afford to lose.
> 2. **Choose the investments you want to make.** There are many different types of investments to choose from, so take some time to think about what's right for you.

3. **Open a brokerage account.** A brokerage account lets you buy and sell stocks, mutual funds, and other securities.
4. **Make regular contributions.** This will help you build your investment portfolio over time.
5. **Stay invested for the long term.** Don't panic and sell your investments if the stock market goes down. The key to successful investing is patience and discipline!

The key to being a successful investor is staying calm and not reacting to short-term market movements. Avoid looking at your investments daily. **Try to think long-term, and you'll be more likely to make intelligent investment decisions.**

As Warren Buffett, one of the most successful investors, says: "Be fearful when others are greedy, and be greedy when others are fearful."

When it comes to investing, there are no guarantees. However, if you're patient and willing to take a little bit of risk, stocks can be a great way to grow your money over time.

Chapter 3

A SIMPLE GUIDE TO RENTING

When you first leave home and get a place of your own, you may decide to rent. Renting a property means you live in a property that belongs to someone else (the landlord). You (the tenant) pay them an agreed fee (the rent), usually monthly or weekly. It's common for you to agree to a specific period for renting and sign a contract (the Lease); for example, most people rent for either a six or 12-month period.

If you plan on renting a property, there are some things you need to know.

What You Need to Know

When renting your first place, you should **do your research** to ensure the property, and the neighborhood fits your lifestyle. **Location is key.** If you like to go out and party, you'll want to live in an area with plenty of nightlife. If you're more of a homebody, opt for a quieter area. Equally, what you might save on rent, you'll spend on transportation costs if you live too far from your work or college.

Another thing to consider is who you'll be living with. Will you be renting alone or with friends?

Renting with friends reduces the cost. For example, if the monthly rent is $2000, splitting it four ways brings each person's cost down to $500 per month. Just ensure everyone sharing the place gets on well together, especially when entering a lease agreement for six months or more.

Renting can be expensive. Make sure you know how much you can afford to spend each month on rent. You'll also need to find out what's included in the rent (e.g., water, electricity, heating) and what isn't (e.g., internet, parking). You'll also need to factor in the cost of a security deposit, which is usually one month's rent.

The security deposit is a way for the landlord to protect themselves if you damage the property or stop paying rent.

If you want to rent a property for $2000 per month, you'll likely have to pay a $2000 security deposit plus $2000 rent upfront before you move in — that's a whopping $4000!

> **Know your Landlord:**
> You may rent from different types of landlords, so it's helpful to know who you're dealing with.
> ▶ **Private landlords** are individuals who own a property and rent them out themselves without any support from a property company or rental agency.

- **College or university landlords** are typically an accommodation team based within the college or university. The team manages properties owned by the university and takes charge of all related rentals.

- A **property agent** is a company that handles real estate professionally for clients. They manage everything related to the property, from finding tenants to fixing any problems that may arise.. Most agents carry out financial background checks on potential tenants.

If You Have a Property in Mind

Once you find a property you like, you first must sign a **lease agreement, pay your security deposit, and then start paying your rent.**

Your landlord will provide you with the written lease agreement before moving in. This document will outline the terms of your rental agreement, such as the rent amount, length of the lease, and any special conditions. It's important to read through the lease agreement carefully and ask questions if you don't understand something. You should also keep a copy to refer to it whenever necessary.

Your landlord may also provide an **inventory list.** This is a list of all the items on the property when you move in, along with their condition. Check the list carefully and note any damage or missing items, so you're not held responsible for them later. The return of your security deposit will hinge on the condition of the property and the inventory list when you leave.

What Happens After You Move in?

When you move into your new place, you should keep the property clean and tidy. This will help you maintain a good relationship with your landlord and avoid penalties. Of course, things may break down sometimes; **if you report them and take responsibility, the landlord will be more understanding.**

As a tenant, **you are responsible for paying your rent on time each month.** If you can't pay the rent, talk to your landlord ASAP—they may be able to work out a payment plan with you. Late payments can result in eviction, so staying on top of your rent is important.

It's also your responsibility to **pay your bills** on time when you live in a property. This includes your electricity, water, internet, and cable bills.

Paying online is often the most straightforward option, but many other options are available.

As soon as you move into a new property, you must arrange to put the **utility bills** in your name. Contact the utility company and provide your name, address and billing details.

You may also wish to arrange extra services, such as cable TV or broadband. Most companies offer package deals that include several services at a discounted price.

Chapter 4

COOKING & FOOD SKILLS

Cooking and food skills are an essential part of life. They can help you save money, stay healthy, and impress your friends and family. Learning basic cooking is a good habit that leads to a lifetime of enjoyment, good food, and healthy eating habits.

This chapter will cover the basics of cooking: cooking different types of foods, reading recipes, and mastering basic skills in the kitchen. With a little bit of practice, you will be able to cook delicious and healthy meals for yourself and your loved ones!

Your Cooking Technique Glossary

There are a few basic cooking techniques that every student chef should know. These techniques will help you prepare different foods and make your dishes look and taste better.

- **Sautéing** is a technique used to cook food quickly in a small amount of oil or butter. To sauté, place the food in a pan over medium-high heat and stir frequently.

- **Braising** is a technique used to simmer meat or vegetables in a small amount of liquid. Place the food in a pan or pot and cover it with liquid to braise. Bring the liquid to a simmer and cook until done.

- **Roasting** is a technique used to cook food in an oven. Place the food on a baking sheet or roasting tray and cook at a high temperature.

- **Blanching** is a technique used to cook vegetables quickly in boiling water. To blanch, place the vegetables in a pot of boiling water and cook for 1-2 minutes. Remove the vegetables with a slotted spoon and put them in ice water to stop cooking.

- **Poaching** is a technique used to cook delicate foods in a liquid such as broth, milk, or wine. To poach, place the food in a poaching pan or pot and bring the water to a simmer. Cook until the desired doneness is reached.

- **Grilling** is a technique used to cook food over an open flame. Place the food on the grill grate and cook until done. Be sure to brush the food with oil or melted butter to help it stay moist and prevent it from sticking to the grate.

Now that you know the basic cooking techniques, you can try cooking various dishes! Be sure to experiment and have fun in the kitchen. With a bit of practice, you will be able to cook like a pro!

Cooking & Food Skills

How to Read a Recipe

A recipe is a set of instructions that tells you how to make a particular dish. It can be helpful to read a recipe through before beginning to cook, so you know what ingredients you will need, what order to prepare the ingredients in, and how long it will take to cook.

When reading a recipe, here are some things to look for:

▸ **The number of servings** the dish will make or serving size

   Serving size refers to the amount of food that a particular recipe will make. Most recipes list the serving size in the header or first paragraph. This is important because it will help you decide how much to make. You may want to halve or quarter the recipe if you are cooking for fewer people.

▸ **What ingredients are needed**

   All recipes list the ingredients needed to make the dish. Check you have all of the ingredients on hand before you start cooking, or you may be running to the store in the middle of making dinner!

▸ **Preparation time**

   Most recipes list how long it will take to prepare the dish. This can help decide what to make for dinner. If you are short on time, choose a recipe that takes less time to prepare or cook.

▶ **Cooking time**

Just like preparation time, **cooking time is listed in most recipes.** This can help you plan your meal. If you have a dish that needs to cook for an hour, you may want to start it early to be ready when you are done cooking everything else.

▶ **What tools and equipment are needed**

Some recipes require special tools or equipment, such as a food processor. **Check what is required before you start.**

▶ **The directions or method**

The directions for a recipe tell you what order to prepare the ingredients and how to cook the dish. They are written in a step-by-step format. Be sure to follow the directions, or you may end up with something that doesn't taste very good!

How to Master Basic Kitchen Skills

Now that you're cooking for yourself and you understand recipes, it's essential to know basic kitchen skills and get the essential tools. Here are a few tips to help you get started.

- **Wash your hands**

    Before doing anything in the kitchen, **wash your hands with soap and warm water.** This will help keep you and your food safe from bacteria.

- **Measuring Ingredients**

    Mastering basic recipes require proper measurement of ingredients. You will need to be familiar with the different types of measuring cups and spoons to do this.

    When measuring liquid ingredients, use a liquid measuring cup or jug. These cups usually have markings on the side to help you calculate the exact amount you need.

    When measuring dry ingredients, be sure to use a dry measuring cup. These cups are typically graduated in ounces or milliliters.

    When measuring solid ingredients, it is best to use a kitchen scale. This will help you get an accurate measurement, especially when dealing with large quantities.

Kitchen Conversion Chart >>>

gr	tsp	tbsp	fl oz	cup	pint	quart	gallon
15	3	1	1/2	1/16	1/32	-	-
28	6	2	1	1/8	1/16	1/32	-
57	12	4	2	1/4	1/8	1/16	-
85	18	6	3	1/3	-	-	-
115	24	8	4	1/2	1/4	1/8	1/32
170	36	12	6	3/4	-	-	-
227	48	16	8	1	1/2	1/4	1/16
908	-	64	32	4	2	1	1/4
-	-	256	128	16	8	4	1

By using the correct type of measuring cup or spoon for the job, you will end up with accurate measurements and successful recipes.

Cooking & Food Skills

▶ **Knives**

A good set of knives is an essential kitchen tool. They will make the preparation of meals much easier and faster.

When choosing knives, look for a set that includes a paring knife, which is suitable for peeling and slicing fruit; a chef's knife, which is suitable for chopping vegetables; and a bread knife, which is used for cutting bread.

Be sure to keep your knives sharpened. A sharp knife is a safe knife.

▸ Cutting Board

Choose a board made from a durable material, such as wood or plastic. Keep your cutting board clean and sanitize it after each use.

Cutting boards come in different colors for different purposes to prevent cross-contamination of bacteria.

- White boards are for bread and dairy (eg. cheese).
- Green boards are for cutting vegetables, fruit and salad.
- Yellow boards are for cutting cooked meat.
- Blue boards are for cutting fish.
- Red boards are for chopping raw meat.

▸ Pots and Pans

Every kitchen needs a good set of pots and pans. When choosing pots and pans, select ones that made from durable materials such as stainless steel or cast iron.

Be sure to choose pots and pans that are the appropriate size for the job. For example, a small saucepan will not be very useful when cooking for a large group of people.

It is also important to have several different sizes of pots and pans on hand. This will give you the flexibility to make a variety of other dishes.

Cooking & Food Skills

▸ **Cooking Utensils**

In addition to pots and pans, you will also need a few basic cooking utensils. These include things like wooden spoons, spatulas, and tongs.

When choosing cooking utensils, look for ones made from durable materials such as stainless steel or wood. These materials will withstand some of the stove's heat and are less likely to melt.

How to Cook on a Budget

Cooking for yourself is usually cheaper than eating out at a restaurant. Here are a few tips to help you stay on budget when cooking independently.

▸ **Plan your meals**

If you plan out your meals for the week, you will be less likely to order takeout or buy food from the grocery store. Planning meals also help you use up all of your ingredients, saving you money.

To plan your meals, simply write out a list of all the meals you want to eat for the week. Then, make a grocery list of all the ingredients you need to make those meals.

- **Cook in bulk**

    If you have time, cook a large batch of food to eat throughout the week. To cook in bulk, simply double or triple the recipe you are making. Once the food is cooked, portion it into individual servings and store it in the fridge or freezer.

    Then just reheat it when you are ready to eat. This will save you time and money since you won't have to cook every day.

- **Shop for bargains at the grocery store sale section**

    Most grocery stores have a section where they sell food on sale, often when it is close to its expiration date. This is a great place to find inexpensive groceries that you can use in your recipes. Check out this section regularly, as you can stock up on staples like grains, pasta, and canned goods when they are on sale. Just ensure you only buy items you will use so they don't go to waste.

- **Avoid processed foods**

    Processed foods are often expensive and not very healthy. Instead, try cooking meals using fresh ingredients. This will save you money, but it will also give you the nutrients your body needs.

- **Use leftovers**

    Don't throw away leftovers from a previous meal! Instead, put them in the fridge and eat them for lunch or dinner the next day.

Cooking & Food Skills

▶ **Compare the prices of different brands**

Not all brands of the same product are created equal. Compare the prices of different brands to find the best deal. Supermarket's own brands are usually cheaper than premium household brands, often with minimal difference in quality.

▶ **Buy in bulk**

If you will use a particular ingredient frequently, buy it in bulk. This will save you money in the long run. Staples such as rice, pasta, and olive oil can often be found at a discount if you buy them in large quantities.

▶ **Make your lunch for college or work**

Making your lunch is a great way to save money and eat healthily. If you brown-bag it, you can save even more money by cooking extra food at dinner and bringing the leftovers for lunch the next day.

How to Store Food

Once you have cooked your meals or bought your groceries, you will need to store the food properly to prevent it from spoiling. Here are a few tips on how to keep food so that it stays fresh:

▸ **Refrigerate perishable items**

Perishable items, such as meat, dairy, and seafood, should be stored in the fridge. These items will go bad quickly at room temperature, so keeping them cold is important. As a simple rule, if the things you bought were in the fridge at the grocery store, they should go back in the fridge when you get home.

▸ **Freeze items for longer storage**

If you aren't using an item right away, you can store it in the freezer. This is a great way to store meat, fish, and vegetables so that they don't go bad. It's also a great way to keep your bulk-cooked meals fresh so you can eat them later. To freeze your food, simply place it in a freezer-safe container and store it in the freezer.

To thaw your food, place it in the fridge the night before you plan to eat it. Always check the food is thawed before cooking.

IMPORTANT: While it is generally ok to thaw foods, cook them and then refreeze the cooked version, it is not recommended to refreeze food that has thawed but not been cooked.

For example: if you have frozen a raw steak, you can defrost it, cook it and then refreeze the cooked steak. However, if you have defrosted the steak and it has been sitting in your fridge for a few days, do not refreeze it.

Cooking & Food Skills

▶ **Store dry goods in a cool, dry place**

Dry goods, such as grains, pasta, and flour, should be stored in a cool, dark place. The pantry is usually the best spot for these items. These items will last for several months when stored properly.

Following these storage tips will help you keep your food fresh and prevent it from spoiling. Just be mindful of expiration dates, as some foods will only last for a short time, even when stored properly.

How to Make a Grocery List

The key to meal planning and saving money is creating a list before going grocery shopping. Lots of people don't do this, and as a result, they often end up buying things they don't need or forgetting items they do need. Planning your meals and creating an organized list is a MUST if you really want to stick to your budget.

Making a list doesn't have to be time consuming if you follow the three golden rules:
- ▶ **Have an ongoing 'we're out of' list** and keep it in an accessible place. As you run low on items, make a quick note of them on your list. This is NOT your actual shopping list, but it will help you compile it. When you decide to buy the item, simply add the item to your shopping list and cross it off the 'we're out of' list.

> ▸ **Keep an inventory** of the items you always need, such as flour, pasta, rice, and oil. While this is time-consuming the first time you do it, your inventory can be maintained easily with a quick weekly update. If you know what you have, it's easier to create both your list and meal plan.
>
> ▸ **Write your weekly meal plan** BEFORE you compile your shopping list. This will help you determine what ingredients you NEED to buy that week.

By following the three golden rules, you can be sure that your list will be comprehensive and efficient—saving you time and money.

When you're ready to write your list, you should look at your meal plan and consider what you may need for each meal. Check your inventory to see what you already have, and write a list of what you need to buy to make each meal. Don't forget to cross-check this with your ongoing 'we're out of' list.

When your list is complete, and you're shopping for your items, don't forget to compare the prices across the different brands to see if you can make savings.

Mastering Basic Recipes

Cooking is all about experimentation. The more you experiment, the better you will become at creating delicious and healthy meals. By mastering a few simple recipes and learning to cook staples, such as eggs, rice, and pasta, you will be able to cook various meals in no time. Here are a few recipes to help get you started.

How to Cook a Mean Breakfast

Breakfast is the most important meal of the day. It kicks starts your metabolism and provides the energy you need to get through the day.

There are endless possibilities for breakfast. Here are a few of our favorites.

Boiled Egg

A soft-boiled egg is a quick and easy breakfast option. Place 1-2 eggs in a pot of boiling water, then cook for 5 minutes. Remove the eggs from the pot with a slotted spoon, then place them in a bowl of cold water.

If you are cooking eggs straight from the fridge, add a minute or two of cooking time.

Omelet

An omelet is a classic breakfast dish that can be made with a variety of different ingredients.

Serves: 1   **Prep Time:** 5mins   **Cooking Time:** 5mins

Ingredients:
- 2-3 Eggs
- Optional Filling — cheese, ham, and vegetables

Directions:
1. Beat 2-3 eggs in a bowl, then pour them into a hot skillet, ensuring they don't burn on the bottom.
2. Cook for 2-3 minutes until the bottom is set, then add your desired fillings. Cheese, ham, and vegetables all make great additions to an omelet.
3. Once you add the fillings, fold the omelet in half and cook for an additional minute or two until the middle is cooked.

Scrambled Eggs

Follow the recipe above and stir the eggs gently with a wooden spoon while cooking to make scrambled eggs. Cook until the eggs are soft-firm.

Pancakes

Pancakes are a delicious way to start your day.

Serves: 8   **Prep time:** 7mins   **Cooking Time:** 10mins

Ingredients:
- 1 Cup of flour
- 2 tablespoons of sugar
- 2 teaspoons of baking powder
- ½ teaspoon of salt

Cooking & Food Skills

- 1 Egg
- 1 Cup of milk
- Optional Toppings!

Directions:
1. Mix 1 cup of flour, 2 tablespoons of sugar, 2 teaspoons of baking powder, and ½ teaspoon of salt in a bowl.
2. Add 1 egg and 1 cup of milk, then mix until the batter is smooth.
3. Pour ¼ cup of batter onto a hot griddle, and cook for 2-3 minutes per side until the pancakes are golden brown.
4. Serve with your favorite toppings, such as maple syrup, jam, or berries.

Breakfast Smoothie

A breakfast smoothie is a great way to combine your favorite fruits and vegetables in one delicious healthy drink.

Serves: 1+   **Prep Time:** 5 mins

Ingredients:
- Fruit or Vegetables — Be creative with what you have!
- ¼ cup of yogurt
- ½ cup of milk

Directions:
Simply blend 1 cup of fresh or frozen fruit, ¼ cup of yogurt, and ½ cup of milk in a blender until thick and creamy. The key with smoothies is to be creative, don't be afraid to combine different fruit, vegetables, and flavor combinations. For example, add a handful of spinach or kale for an extra boost of nutrients.

Life Skills for Young Adults

Easy Main Meals

Main meals are important too, and there's no reason they can't be quick and easy. By mastering one or two simple sauces, you can adapt them to make various dishes. Here are a few simple recipes to get you started:

Pasta with Tomato Sauce

Tomato sauce is a versatile sauce you can use in various dishes.

Serves: 4   **Prep Time:** 5mins   **Cooking Time:** 15mins

Ingredients:
- 1 Onion, chopped
- 2 Garlic cloves, chopped
- 1 Can of diced tomatoes
- 1 teaspoon of sugar
- 1 tablespoon of herbs — such as basil or oregano
- Salt & Pepper to taste
- Pasta

Directions:
1. Sauté 1 chopped onion and 2 cloves of garlic in a tablespoon of olive oil until softened.
2. Add 1 can of diced tomatoes, 1 teaspoon of sugar, and 1 tablespoon of chopped fresh herbs, such as basil or oregano.
3. Simmer the sauce for 15 minutes, then season to taste with salt and pepper.

4. In the meantime, to cook the perfect pasta, bring a pot of water to the boil, then add 1 tablespoon of salt. Add the pasta and cook for 2-3 minutes less than the instructions on the packet. Drain the pasta, then add it to the tomato sauce. Serve with grated cheese and a side salad.

Taco Meat Sauce

Taco meat is another versatile sauce you can use in various dishes, such as tacos, burritos, or nachos. You can also use it as a topping for salads or pasta dishes. If you don't have the individual spices, replace them with a packet of taco seasoning.

Serves: 4   **Prep Time:** 5mins   **Cooking Time:** 10mins

Ingredients:
- 1 chopped onion
- 1 chopped garlic clove
- 1 pound of ground beef
- 1 can of diced tomatoes
- 1 teaspoon of chilli powder
- 1 teaspoon of cumin
- Salt and pepper to taste
- Taco shells or tortillas
- Optional extras: shredded cheese, lettuce & sour cream

Directions:
1. Saute 1 chopped onion and 1 crushed garlic clove in a tablespoon of olive oil until they are soft.

2. Add 1 pound of ground beef to the onion and garlic mixture, breaking it up as you add it. Fry on medium heat until the meat has browned (keep turning it and do not let it burn).
3. Drain any excess fat, then add a can of diced tomatoes, a teaspoon of chili powder, and a teaspoon of cumin. If you like your chili hot, add more chili powder or fresh chilis according to taste.
4. Season with salt and pepper to taste.
5. Simmer for 10 minutes, add to taco shells or tortillas and serve with shredded cheese, lettuce, and sour cream.

Meat Free Vegetarian Option

If you want to create a vegetarian or vegan option, simply replace the ground beef with a meat substitute. Suitable meat substitutes include using a vegan mince replacement, or you could use grated carrot, finely sliced celery, red lentils or shredded cabbage instead.

15min Soup with Leftovers

Soups can make a healthy and nutritious meal. They are quick and easy and can contain almost anything, and are a great way to use up your leftovers.

Serves: 4   **Prep Time:** 10mins   **Cooking Time:** 25mins

Ingredients:
Any vegetables you have available or any leftovers from other meals — chop them up into small cubes.

- Two bouillon cubes
- Chopped garlic or onion (optional)

Directions:
1. Saute your prepared vegetables in a saucepan for 5-10 minutes
2. Add water to the pan, enough to cover the vegetables
3. Bring to the boil, and sprinkle in the bouillon cubes
4. Stir well and turn down the heat
5. Simmer for 10-15 minutes or until the vegetables are soft
6. Add salt and pepper to taste
7. Serve (with bread if you wish)!

5 Ways to Spruce up Your Soup

▸ To turn your soup into a broth, add two tablespoons of dried broth mix (red lentils and barley)

▸ Add pasta to your soup, if you want a more filling meal

▸ You can also add any leftover meat to your soup, such as chicken, bacon, and beef if you prefer a meaty flavor—make sure you heat through thoroughly before serving.

▸ Spice up your soup by adding a sprinkling of chili powder, curry powder or paste, or cumin seeds

▸ Combination of ingredients that make great soup

- Butternut squash, potato, onion, and a teaspoon of curry powder for spicy butternut squash soup
- Leek and potatoes work well, along with bacon (optional). This works well as a thicker soup, so be sure to add the corn starch mix mentioned above.
- Broth mix, peas, carrots, onion, and diced peeled potatoes make an excellent broth, and again, the corn start mix makes it thicker and creamy, especially if you use milk instead of water. Chicken or lamb leftovers are great additions to any broth!

Chapter 5

LIVING A HEALTHY LIFESTYLE & CARING FOR YOUR MENTAL HEALTH

Living a healthy lifestyle is vital for your physical and mental health. It's important to ensure you take care of your own individual needs so you have the energy to allow yourself to live the life you want. As well as feeling better, if you eat healthily and take regular exercise, you will be at lower risk of developing health conditions in the future. You'll also find that you build up your immune system and are more likely to quickly get over sickness, bugs and viruses.

When we eat and drink, our bodies take in energy from our consumption; we measure this in calories. We need this energy to keep us alive and to keep our bodies running in an efficient, healthy way.

Our bodies use energy for everything from breathing, circulating blood to digesting food. Even when you're asleep or resting, your body is still using energy to maintain its vital functions.

Calories are just units of measurement that we use to track the amount of energy we are taking in from food and drink, and the amount of energy we are using through activity.

The recommended daily intake (RDI) of calories for men is 2,500, and for women, it is 2,000. However, this will vary depending on age, weight, height, and activity level.

For example, a person who works as a sports coach has a physical job, and therefore they are more likely to need more calories than a person who works in an office. Of course, using our brainpower requires energy, so that person would still need their fair share of calories.

The most important thing you can do is **make sure you're eating a healthy and balanced diet of nutritious foods from all the food groups.**

How to Get the Energy Your Body Needs

The body derives calories (energy) from nutrients. The three primary nutrients that provide energy are:

Living a Healthy Lifestyle & Caring for Your Mental Health

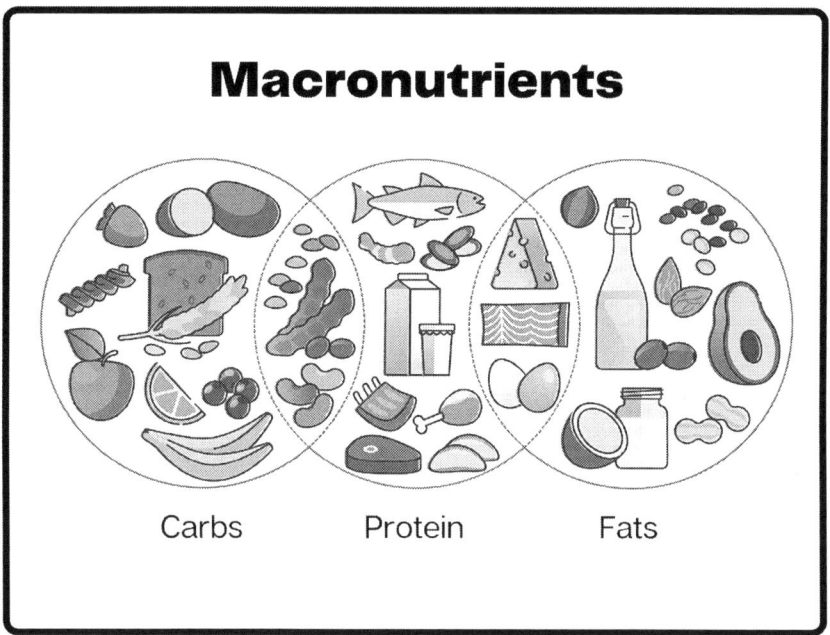

- **Carbohydrates. Carbs are broken down into glucose, which the body uses for energy.** They are commonly found in grains, bread, pasta, rice, potatoes, fruit, vegetables and cereals. They are also found in sugary foods such as candy, cake, and cookies.

- **Fats. Fats are a concentrated source of energy** and are needed for other functions in the body, such as making hormones, cell membranes, and breaking down other nutrients. For example, Fat is a source of fatty acid that helps the body absorb vitamins A, D, and E. The body cannot produce fatty acids itself, so our bodies would be unable to absorb these without any fat.

Therefore, a small amount of fat is required as part of a healthy diet, but too much can lead to health problems.

The two primary fats found in food are saturated fats and unsaturated fats.

- **Saturated fats.** Saturated fats are found in animal products such as butter, cream, meat, and cheese. They can also be in some plant oils such as coconut oil, palm oil, and cocoa butter.
- **Unsaturated fats.** Unsaturated fats are found in plant oils such as olive oil, rapeseed oil, sunflower oil, and soya bean oil. They are also in oily fish such as salmon, mackerel, and herring. Unlike saturated fats, 'good' unsaturated fats can help reduce your cholesterol levels and lower your risk of developing heart problems.

- **Proteins. Proteins are needed to grow and repair your body tissues.** Your body breaks down protein into amino acids, which are the building blocks of your muscles. Proteins are found in meat, fish, eggs, beans, and lentils. They are also in dairy products such as milk and cheese.

As well as carbs, fats, and protein, the body also needs micro-nutrients in vitamins and minerals.

Essential Vitamins and Minerals

Vitamins and minerals are essential nutrients needed in small amounts to keep the body healthy and functioning correctly. These nutrients are in various foods, including fruits, vegetables, whole grains, dairy products, and meat. While most of us get enough nutrients if we eat a balanced diet, occasionally, we need to take supplements.

There are several types of vitamins and minerals, but we'll explore some of the most common below:

- **Vitamin A** is in cheese, eggs, oily fish, milk, and yogurt. It helps your body fight infections and illness, helps to keep your skin healthy, and is also good for vision.

- There are many different types of **vitamin B.** The role of B vitamins is to help release energy from the food we eat. They are also crucial for our body's general health and wellbeing.

- **Vitamin C** is in citrus fruits, tomatoes, peppers, broccoli, and Brussels sprouts. It helps to protect cells and keeps them healthy.

- **Vitamin D** is in oily fish, eggs, and fortified foods such as cereals and fat spreads. It helps the body absorb calcium, required for healthy bones and teeth.

- **Vitamin E** is in vegetable oils, nuts, and seeds. It helps to protect cells from damage.

- **Calcium** is in dairy products such as milk, cheese, and yogurt. It is also in green leafy vegetables, such as broccoli and cabbage. Calcium is needed for healthy bones and teeth.

- **Iron** is in meat, poultry, fish, beans, lentils, and fortified cereals. It helps make red blood cells, which carry oxygen around the body.

Essential Vitamins

Vitamin A	
Vitamin B1	
Vitamin B2	
Vitamin B3	
Vitamin E	
Vitamin K	
Vitamin H	
Vitamin C	

How to Eat a Healthy and Balanced Diet

A healthy and balanced diet includes a variety of nutrient-rich foods your body needs to function so that you feel your best, have good energy levels, and maintain your health.

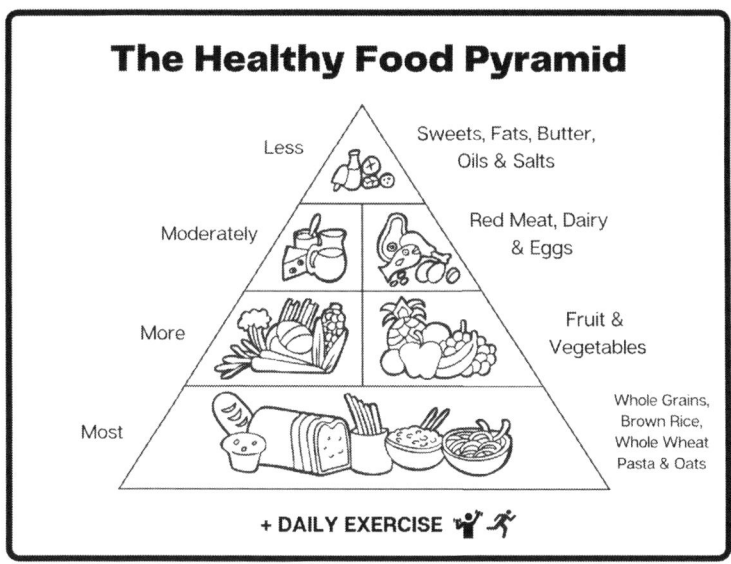

A healthy diet should consist of all the food groups:

▶ **Fruit and vegetables:** you should aim to eat at least five portions of various fruit and vegetables each day. This is because they are a good source of vitamins and minerals and dietary fiber.

▶ **Starchy foods and Carbohydrates:** provide a good base of carbohydrates for your meals and are high in fiber. You should eat starchy foods such as potatoes, brown rice, whole wheat pasta, and whole grain bread.

- **Protein:** include a **variety of meat, fish, beans, and lentils** in your diet as they are rich in protein and other nutrients.

- **Dairy:** dairy products such as milk, cheese, and yogurt provide calcium which is essential for strong bones and teeth

- **Fats:** oils and spreads provide essential fatty acids and are a good energy source.

Remember that **we all have different energy needs depending on age, gender, activity levels, and weight.**

When it comes to portion sizes, a good rule of thumb is to fill up around one-third of your plate with Carbs, one-third with vegetables or salad, and the final third with meat, fish, or beans.

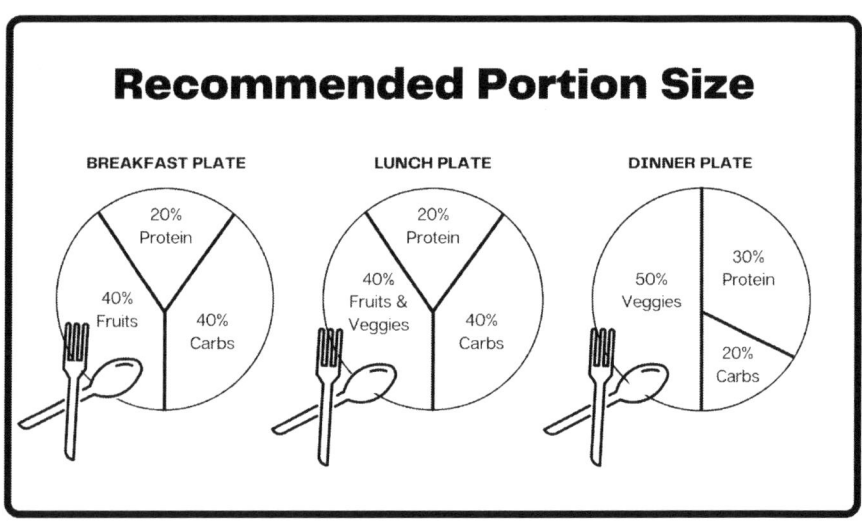

Water and Hydration

Water is essential for having a healthy body and mind. **Every single cell in our bodies needs water to function correctly.** Water helps transport oxygen and nutrients around the body, regulates our body temperature, protects our organs, and aids digestion.

We need to drink around eight glasses of water per day to stay hydrated. To ensure you are getting enough water, try to drink a glass of water with every meal and snack. You can also carry a water bottle with you when you are out and about. Your daily recommended daily intake can be met by drinking fluids, eating water-rich foods such as fruits and vegetables, and from the water found in other drinks such as tea and coffee.

Avoid sugary or fizzy drinks, as they can cause tooth decay, and the sugar can give you an energy high followed by an energy low. Try to stick to water or other unsweetened drinks.

How to Read Food Labels

Food labels contain valuable information that can help you make healthier choices. Here are some things to look out for:

▸ **The list of ingredients:** tells you what is in the food. The first ingredient listed is usually the main one, and the last ingredient listed is typically present in smaller amounts. So if sugar is one of the first few ingredients, then the food is high in sugar.

- **The nutrition information panel:** gives you information on the energy (calories), fat, saturates, sugar, and salt content of the food. It is important to remember that the serving size listed on the label is not necessarily the same as the portion size you would eat. For example, a packet of biscuits may say that it contains eight servings, but if you eat the whole pack, you would need to multiply the nutrition information by 8.

- **The % Reference Intake (RI):** tells you the percentage of an adult's recommended daily intake provided by one serving of the food. For example, if a product contains 20% of the RI for sugar, one serving provides 20% of the sugar an adult should eat in a day.

- **The use-by date:** gives the date up to which you can use the food without it going off.

Of course, the importance of diet and nutrition is only one part of the puzzle when staying healthy. Being physically active, getting enough sleep, and managing stress are important factors.

Living a Healthy Lifestyle & Caring for Your Mental Health

THE IMPORTANCE OF SLEEP:

Getting enough sleep is important for your physical and mental health. It's when your body repairs and restores itself, and it's also when your brain consolidates important information.

Most people need around 7–8 hours of sleep per night.

If you are finding it difficult to get enough sleep, there are a few things you can try, such as:

Create a relaxing environment in your bedroom.

Make sure the room is dark, quiet, and cool, and that your bed is comfortable.

Remove distractions from your bedroom.

Reserve your bedroom for sleep, and try to avoid working or using electronic devices in bed.

Establish a regular bedtime routine.

Try to go to bed and get up at the same time every day and have a routine for getting ready each morning. You may prefer to have a shower each morning before you get dressed.

How to Stay Fit

Taking part in regular exercise is important for your physical health and well-being. It can help to reduce your risk of developing health conditions. It can also help keep your weight under control and improve your mental health and mood.

You should aim to participate in two types of exercise: aerobic exercise and strength training.

- **Aerobic exercise:** aerobic exercise is any activity that gets your heart rate up and makes you breathe more heavily. It includes activities such as walking, running, swimming, and biking. Aerobic exercise helps to improve your cardiovascular fitness and can also help reduce stress and anxiety.

- **Strength training:** strength training is any activity that works your muscles and helps to improve your muscle strength. It includes activities such as lifting weights and doing bodyweight exercises. Strength training helps to improve your bone density and can also help reduce the risk of injuries.

The best way to stay fit is to be physically active every day. Adults should aim for at least 30 minutes of moderate-intensity physical activity on most, if not all, days of the week. Moderate-intensity activities include walking, swimming, and cycling. You can also do a combination of different activities to reach your daily goal.

If you are not used to being physically active, start slowly and build up gradually. For example, you could start with 10 minutes of walking every day and then increase this by 5 minutes each week until you reach 30 minutes.

The benefits of regular exercise extend far beyond weight control. Exercise can also help reduce the risk of developing conditions such as heart disease, strokes, type 2 diabetes, some types of cancer, and osteoporosis. It can also help to improve mental health, including reducing stress, anxiety, and depression.

How to Cope with Emotions

To remain healthy, you also need to manage your feelings in a healthy way. We all know that there are ups and downs in life. There are times we handle heart-breaking moments and glorious ones too. We need to be ready to handle disappointments, stress, and times of crisis. People who don't have healthy coping skills often develop unhealthy ones.

How to Deal with Stress

Stress is our body's response to demands placed on it. It is a normal human emotion that we all experience from time to time.

The best way to describe stress is to imagine you have a bucket inside your body that collects your everyday stresses.

Life Skills for Young Adults

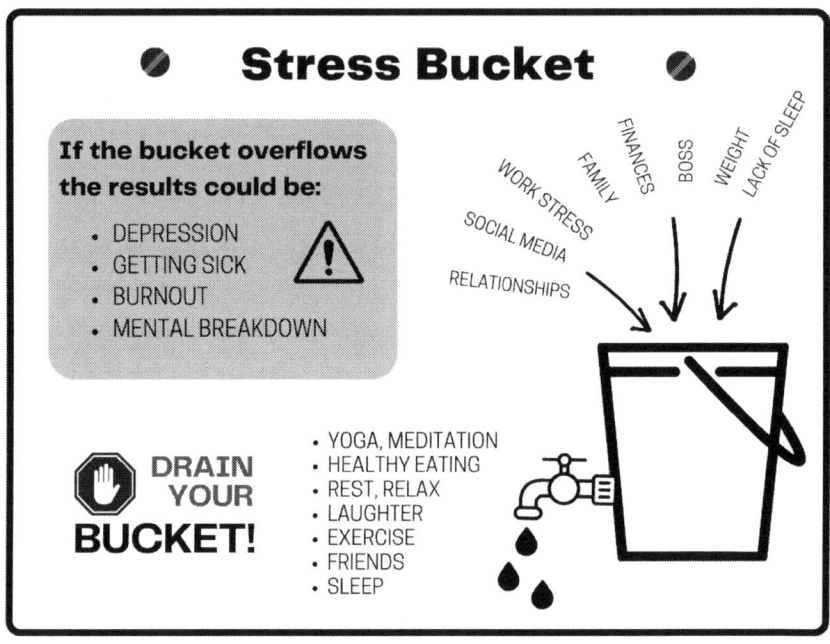

Your bucket fills with stresses about work, finances, home life, relationships, and health. We all have a different sized bucket, and we all manage stress differently, so something you see as being stressful, another person will not, and vice-versa. When many things happen, our bucket fills, causing us to feel anxious, tired, low and emotional, burnt out, and snappy or irritable. When we begin to feel like this, we must relieve the stress by turning on a tap and letting some of it out, or the bucket will overflow, and we will become unwell.

There are many different ways to let stress out of our buckets. Some people exercise, meditate or do yoga, some take long baths, listen to music or read books—there is no one right way to do it. Try to find what works for you and do it regularly before your bucket begins to overflow.

Here are some tips on how to empty your stress bucket:

1. **Exercise** — this can be anything from a brisk walk to a more intense workout at the gym. It releases endorphins which have mood-boosting effects.
2. **Relaxation techniques** — such as yoga, meditation, or deep breathing.
3. **Connect with nature** — go for a walk in the park, sit in the garden or spend time near the water.
4. **Spend time with loved ones** — positive social interactions can help reduce stress levels.
5. **Do something you enjoy** — reading, cooking, painting, or another hobby.
6. **Get a massage** — this can help relax the muscles and ease tension.
7. **Make time for yourself** — even if it's just 10 minutes a day, make sure you have some "me time" to do something you enjoy.
8. **Be assertive** — say "no" to things that you don't want to do or that will cause you undue stress.
9. **Learn to accept the things you can't change** — this can be difficult, but holding onto resentment and frustration will only add to your stress levels.
10. **Seek professional help** — if your stress levels are impacting your day-to-day life, it may be time to seek help from a therapist or counselor.

Do whatever you need to do to let the stress out of your bucket!

Talk about it!

The more we learn to talk about how we feel, the better our mental health can be. This isn't a sign of weakness. It's empowering as it helps you take control of your wellbeing.

We all have disappointments and crisis points in our lives, so it's natural to feel down, anxious, or stressed from time to time. It's when these feelings become prolonged and begin to impact your daily life that they become a problem. **Talking about how you feel can be the first step in managing stress, anxiety, or depression.**

Remember, **you are not alone.** Feeling stressed, disappointed, or in crisis is common, and many people feel just like you do. There is no shame in seeking help. **Talk to a trusted friend or family member, your doctor, a counselor, or a therapist.** The sooner you reach out for help, the sooner you can begin to feel better and move on.

Chapter 6

PERSONAL HEALTHCARE & BASIC FIRST AID

Most young adults are healthy and don't have to think about their health very much. However, it's important to be proactive about your health and know how to take care of yourself if you become ill. This chapter will teach you the basics of accessing healthcare and administering first aid.

While every effort is made to ensure the information here is accurate, it is for general information only and is not intended, nor should it be taken as medical advice. Please consult a doctor or other healthcare professional for any specific health-related advice.

Healthcare in the United States

The healthcare system in the United States can be confusing, but you have many options available as a young adult. Below, we outline some of the key healthcare resources and options available to you:

▶ **Choosing Not to have Insurance**

Choosing not to have insurance (or being uninsured) is your choice, but be aware that in certain States, **you may be penalized** at the end of the year on your taxes. The penalties vary by State, so check your local laws if you need to file an exemption or not. In addition, healthcare costs are often much higher for those without insurance, so you may end up paying a lot out of pocket if you need to go to the doctor or hospital.

▶ **Healthcare through your parents' insurance**

If you are under 26, **check your parents' insurance** as you may have coverage under their plan. This just requires a quick phone call to your parents' provider.

▶ **Healthcare through your School**

Some Colleges offer students healthcare insurance while attending the university. This option is typically for international students, but some colleges also offer it to Stateside students. **Talk to your college to get more details.**

In addition, most colleges offer discounted health care services to their students on campus. These services typically include check-ups, prescriptions, and some specialist care. Again check with your college the level of services on offer.

▸ **Getting Insurance Through Your Employer**

Most employers offer health insurance for full-time employees. In most cases, this is either free (if your employer pays the whole premium) or more affordable (if you have to pay part of the premium) than finding your insurance. There are often other added benefits such as reduced cost or even free eye or dental care. However, if you lose or leave your job, you will lose this health plan.

▸ **Getting Insurance Through the Government (Medicaid/Medicare)**

If you cannot afford private health insurance, you may be eligible for Medicaid or Medicare. Both programs offer a wide range of medical services, including doctor's visits, hospital stays, emergency care, and prescription medications. To find out if you qualify for these programs, you should speak to your state Department of Health Services or visit their website.

▸ **Getting Insurance Through a Private Company**

You get this **health care on your own through any private health insurance company** you wish. It allows for more tailoring to your needs than any other plans but can be costly.

When Can I Get Insurance?

In most cases, you can only enroll for insurance during an "open enrollment period" or if you have a "qualifying life event."

"Open Season/Enrollment" refers to a period each year when you can enroll in a new health plan or update existing plans. This varies State by State but tends to be at the end of each year. You can sign up for a healthcare plan from a private healthcare provider during this period. You can find information on health insurance plans in your state with a simple google search.

Before signing up, **it's a good to consider what coverage you may need for the coming year.** For example, if you plan on having a baby, you will want to make sure your plan covers maternity care.

You can only sign up for a health insurance plan outside of the open enrollment period if you have a qualifying life event. Events include getting married, having a baby, or losing your job.

Once you have your health plan, it can take anywhere from 2 weeks to 90 days to activate. This time frame is referred to as a gap in coverage. If you require medical attention during this time, your health plan may not reimburse the cost. Check the terms and policies of your plan for specific details.

Seeing a Doctor

Firstly, you need to find out if a doctor is 'in your network.' **Your insurance company will have a list of doctors that you can see,** called in-network doctors. If you see a doctor who is not on this list, it is called an out-of-network doctor. Going to see an out-of-network doctor will usually cost you more money.

If you do not have health insurance, you will have to pay for your healthcare yourself. You can still go to the doctor, but it will cost you more money.

New Patient Intake or Walk-In

If you have never seen the doctor before, you need to do a new patient intake. This is where the doctor will ask you questions about your medical history and your current health. They will also likely ask for your medical history, insurance, and financial information. To make a doctor your PCP (Primary care physician), **you will usually need to make the New Patient appointment,** call your insurance and list that Doctor as your PCP.

If you have seen the doctor before, you can usually just make a walk-in appointment.

PCP Vs. Urgent Care Vs. Specialist Vs ER

You will usually see your primary care physician (PCP) if you have a general health concern. If you have a specific health concern, you may be referred by your PCP to a specialist. For example, if you have a heart condition, you will see a cardiologist.

Urgent care is for when you need to see a doctor, but it is not an emergency. For example, if you have an earache and need medicine for it, but you can't see your doctor for two days. It's not severe enough for the ER, but the pain is too much for a two-day wait. The emergency room is for when you need to see a doctor right away for an emergency.

How to Register with a Local Doctor in the UK

In the UK, you should register for a doctor when you move into a new area. You can register with any GP (general practitioner) in your area, even if they are not your local surgery. You will need to fill out a registration form, which you can get from your surgery or online. You will need to provide your contact details, date of birth, and National Insurance number. Once you have registered, your GP is your first port of call for all your healthcare needs.

How to Make an Appointment with a GP in the UK

If you need to see a GP, you can call your surgery or go online to book an appointment. You will usually be able to see a GP the same day if it's an emergency. If it's not an emergency, you will can make an appointment, usually within a couple of weeks.

How to Perform Basic First Aid

Being able to perform basic first aid is an important life skill.

First aid is the initial care given to someone who is injured or suddenly unwell. This could be anything from a minor cut or bruise to a more severe injury such as a broken bone. First aid should be given as soon as possible after the injury or illness. It is not a substitute for professional medical care, but it can often help to stabilize the patient until help arrives.

Let's explore some common first aid scenarios and what you can do to help.

How to Deal with Cuts and Grazes

If you have a cut or graze, you should clean the wound as soon as possible to prevent infection.

1. **Rinse the wound** with clean water for several minutes.
2. **Apply pressure** if the bleeding is constant.
3. To prevent infection of the wounded area, **apply an antiseptic cream** or ointment per the manufacturer's instructions if you can.
4. **Place a sterile dressing over the wound** and secure it with adhesive tape or a bandage.

5. If the bleeding is constant and does not stop after 10 minutes of applying pressure, **seek medical attention** immediately.

How to Treat a Burn

Burn injuries are common and can range from mild to severe. Burns occur when your skin comes into contact with a heat source, such as boiling water or a hot stove.

While minor burns are treatable; it's advisable to see a medical professional for more serious injuries.

1. For minor burns, **hold the affected area under cool running water for at least 10 minutes** to reduce swelling. Avoid applying ice or anything ice-cold, which could further damage the skin. You should also avoid greasy substances or creams.
2. **Seek medical attention** immediately if the burn is severe or if it covers a large area of skin.
3. For all burns, **avoid breaking any blisters** that have formed, as this could lead to infection.

How to Remove a Splinter

Splinters are also common injuries and can usually be removed easily. If left, they can cause infections under the skin. Therefore, it's important to remove splinters in the safest, cleanest way. To do this, you should follow the steps below:

1. **Clean the area** around the splinter with warm water and soap.
2. **Use a needle or tweezers** to remove the splinter carefully.
3. If the splinter is embedded deeply, **seek medical attention.**
4. **Apply an antiseptic cream or ointment** to the area and cover it with a sterile dressing.
5. **Change the dressing regularly** to prevent infection.

How to Deal with Fainting

Fainting occurs when you lose consciousness for a short time, usually due to a drop in blood pressure. It is caused by several things, including low blood sugar levels, standing for a long time, or the sight of blood. It can also be a symptom of an underlying medical condition.

If someone faints, try to revive them and then seek medical attention if they do not regain consciousness.

1. **Lie them down on their back and raise their legs** above heart level. This will help to increase blood flow to the brain.
2. **Give them plenty of space,** reassure them and have them sit up slowly.
3. If they do not regain consciousness, **seek medical attention** immediately.

How to Deal with Choking

Choking occurs when an object becomes lodged in your throat or windpipe, blocking airflow. Choking is a common medical emergency, but it can also be very scary. If someone is choking, it is important to act quickly and try to dislodge the object.

1. **Encourage them to cough**—this may help dislodge the object.
2. **Give the person up to five back blows** between their shoulder blades with the heel of your hand.
   To perform back blows, you should:
   - Place one arm around the person's chest, bend them over at the waist
   - Give 5 blows to the back using the bottom of your hand, striking in between the shoulder blades.
3. If this does not work, **try up to five abdominal thrusts** (also known as the Heimlich maneuver)
   To perform the Heimlich maneuver, you should:
   - Stand behind the person who is choking, with one foot in front the other to help you balance (if it's a child, you may need to kneel).
   - Place your arms around their waist, and tilt them forward slightly
   - Make a fist with one of your hands and place it just above the navel of the person.
   - With the other hand, grab the fist and then thrust this into the stomach with a quick, upward movement, just as if you're trying to pick the person up.
   - Repeat five times
4. Repeat these steps until the object is dislodged.
5. **Seek medical attention** if they are still choking or become unconscious.

Personal Healthcare & Basic First Aid

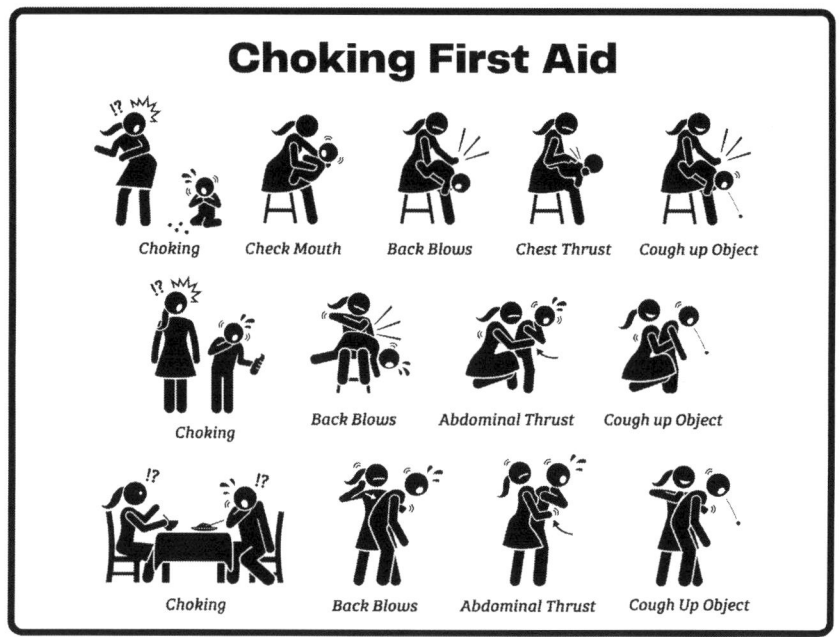

How to Deal with a Sprain or Broken Bone

A sprain occurs when you stretch or tear a ligament—the tissue that connects bones. A broken bone occurs when your bone is either cracked or broken entirely. Both injuries can be extremely painful and require treatment immediately.

It's important to remember that **a broken bone always requires medical attention.** A doctor understands how the bones heal and work and will provide you with the best advice for such an injury.

If you think someone has broken bone, follow these steps:

1. **Assess the situation.** Do you need to phone an ambulance, or can the person be taken to an accident and emergency facility?
2. If possible, **immobilize the injured limb** with a sling or splint to prevent further damage.
3. **Seek medical attention** as soon as possible.

If you think someone has **sprained** their ankle, wrist, or knee, follow these steps:

1. **Apply ice** to the area for 20 minutes every two hours. If you don't have an ice pack, a pack of frozen peas will do.
2. **Keep the injured limb elevated** above heart level to reduce swelling.
3. Take over-the-counter anti inflammatory medication, if you are able to, ensuring you follow the instructions as prescribed by your doctor.
4. **Seek medical attention** if the pain does not improve within 48 hours or if there is severe swelling, bruising, or any deformity.

How to Put Someone in the Recovery Position

If someone is unconscious but breathing, you should place them in the recovery position. This will help keep the airway clear and prevent choking on vomit or inhaling their tongue.

1. Kneel on the floor, next to the person lying on their back.
2. Extend the arm that is closest to you at a right angle to their body with their palm facing up.
3. Fold the other arm so the back of their hand rests on the cheek closest to you.

Personal Healthcare & Basic First Aid

4. Bend the person's knee farthest away from you, and carefully roll them onto their side by pulling the bent knee towards you. The bent knee should be at a right angle.
5. Their bent arm should be supporting their head, while their extended arm will prevent you from rolling them too much.
6. Tilt-back their head, lift their chin, and check that nothing is blocking their airway.
7. Stay with them, and monitor their condition until help has arrived.

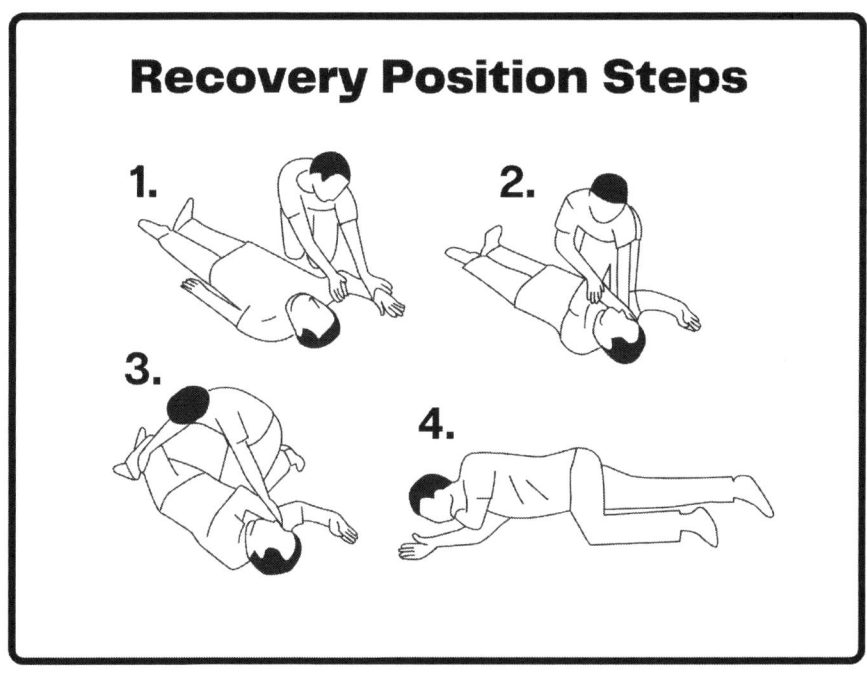

How to Build a First Aid Kit

A first aid kit is an essential item to have in your home, as it contains all the supplies you need to deal with minor injuries and illnesses. While you can buy complete sets, it can be helpful to build your first aid kit so that you can tailor it to your specific needs.

Here are some essential **items to include in your first aid kit:**

- A range of Band-Aids (different shapes and sizes)
- Small, medium, and large gauge dressings—make sure they are sterile
- Triangular bandages
- Bandages and gauze
- Adhesive tape
- Antiseptic wipes or cream
- Painkillers
- A thermometer
- Tweezers
- Medical Scissors
- A first aid manual
- Cream or spray to relieve bites and stings
- Antihistamines

If you have any specific medical conditions, include any medication or supplies you need. It is also a good idea to keep a list of emergency phone numbers in your kit and copies of important medical documents such as your insurance card.

Chapter 7

MAINTAINING RELATIONSHIPS: SOCIAL SKILLS, NETWORKING, AND COMMUNICATION

One of the most important things you will do in your life is to build and maintain relationships. This includes **family, friends, partners, and work colleagues.** The people close to you will have a significant impact on your life, so it is important to nurture your relationships. This means making time for the people in your life, communicating effectively, and constructively resolving conflicts.

Building Relationships

How to Make an Excellent First Impression

The first step to building any kind of relationship is to make an excellent first impression. Whether it's a first date, a job interview, or meeting your future in-laws, you want to make sure that you put your best foot forward.

This means **being polite and friendly,** dressing appropriately, and **arriving on time.** Remember, a smile goes a long way. Greeting someone with a smile and making eye contact shows that you are interested in them and open to communication. **Being positive and upbeat** will also make you more likable.

If you are shy or introverted, it can be helpful to **have some conversation starters in mind.** This way, you won't be caught off-guard if there is a lull in the conversation. Typical conversation starters include asking about their day, discussing current events, or discussing mutual interests.

Finally, **don't forget your manners,** both in-person and online. Saying please and thank you, holding the door open for someone, or sending a thank you card after receiving a gift are all good manners. **These small gestures make you memorable** and show that you considerate others and appreciate their efforts.

How to Remember a Name

The chances are you know someone good at remembering names. They can meet someone new and recall their name days, weeks, or even years later. While some people are naturally good at this, remembering names is like any other skill—it can be learned and practiced.

Maintaining Relationships: Social Skills, Networking, and Communication

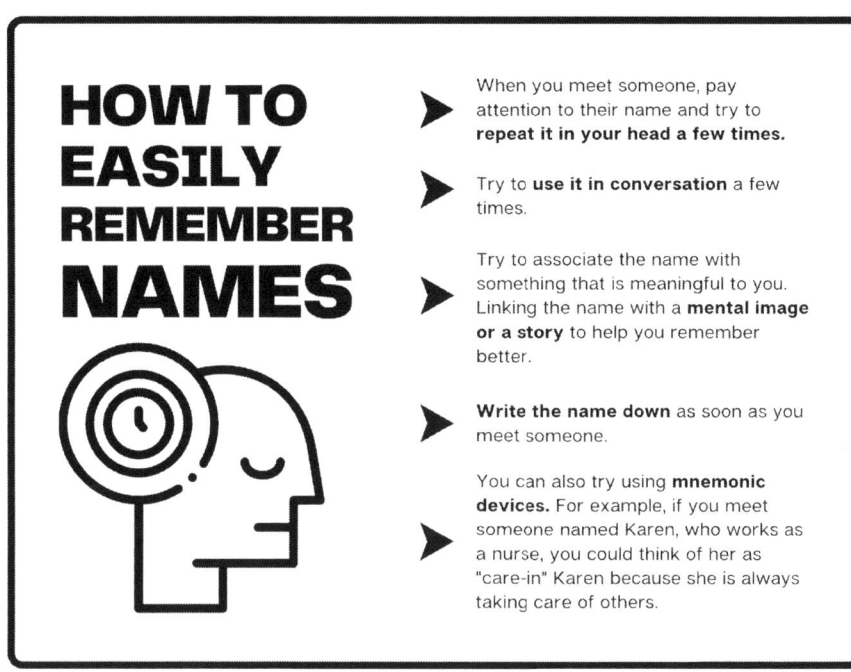

One of the reasons remembering names is so tricky is that we are bombarded with so much information every day. We are constantly meeting new people, and our brains can only process so much information at one time. This is why you should always make an effort to focus when you meet someone new.

When you meet someone, pay attention to their name and **try to repeat it in your head a few times.** It can also be helpful to repeat their name back to them or **use it in conversation** a few times. Try to **associate the name with something** meaningful to you and already imprinted in your brain. For example, if you meet someone named Harry, you could think of the story of Harry Potter. Linking the name with a mental image or a story will help you remember it better.

Another tip for remembering names is to **write them down** as soon as you meet someone. This way, you will have a visual reminder of the person's name and can refer back to it if you forget.

You can also try using mnemonic devices, which are methods for remembering information that **links the information to something else** that is easier to remember. For example, if you meet Karen, who works as a nurse, you could think of her as "care-in" Karen because she is always taking care of others.

Finally, don't get discouraged if you forget a name or two. It happens to everyone. Just apologize and move on. The important thing is to make an effort to remember the names of the people you meet.

Now that you've mastered first impressions and remembering names, it's time to move on to the next step—strengthening relationships.

Strengthening Relationships

How to Listen Effectively

Listening is one of the most important skills you can develop, personally and professionally. **Much of what you learn in life is through listening.** When you listen, you can gather information, understand other points of view, and build relationships.

When you are listening to someone, it shows. You make eye contact, nod your head and give them verbal cues that you are engaged in the conversation. You might even find yourself mirroring their body language.

Active listening can be difficult, especially if you are tired or distracted. However, it is important to make an effort to listen to what the other person is saying. This means not just hearing the words but also understanding the meaning behind them.

There are a few things you can do to be a better listener. First, make sure that you **give the other person your full attention.** This means putting away your phone, making eye contact, and maintaining an open body position.

Second, try to **resist the urge to interrupt.** It can be tempting to jump in and share your own opinion, but try to let the other person finish what they're saying.

Third, **paraphrase what the other person has said** to make sure you understand. This involves repeating back what you have heard in your own words. For example, you could say, "So you're saying that you're feeling overwhelmed by your workload."

Finally, **ask questions.** This shows that you are interested in what the other person is saying and want to know more. Listen twice as much as you talk, and give the other person your full attention.

Now that you've learned the basics of communication, it's time to move on to the next skill—teamwork.

How to Work in a Team

Working in a team can be a great way to accomplish more than you could on your own. It also allows you to share the load, delegate tasks and build relationships.

However, teamwork doesn't always come naturally. It can be challenging to learn how to work effectively with others, especially if you are used to working alone.

You can do a few things to be a better team member. First, **be a good communicator.** This means being able to listen to others, share your ideas, and compromise when necessary.

Second, you need to **be able to take direction.** This doesn't mean that you have to do everything that your team leader says, but be open to input from others.

Third, you need to **be able to work with different types of people.** This means understanding and respecting the differences in others, even if you don't always agree with them.

Fourth, **be flexible.** Things change all the time in a team environment, so you need to be able to adapt to new situations.

Finally, you need to **be able to work under pressure.** This means meeting deadlines, handling stress, and staying calm in difficult situations.

If you can master the art of teamwork, you'll be well on your way to success in any field.

How to Build Your Network

With the advent of social media, networking and communication have become easier than ever before. However, there is still an art to building relationships and communicating effectively.

If you want **to build a strong network, try to be active and engaged.** This means participating in conversations, sharing your own experiences and thoughts, and being supportive of others. It is also important to be genuine and authentic in your interactions. People can see through phony behavior, and it is hard to build trust with someone if you are not being authentic.

In addition to being active and engaged, **be helpful.** When you are helpful, people are more likely to want to help you. Offer your expertise and advice freely, and be willing to **go out of your way to assist others.** Remember, what goes around comes around.

Keep a list of people you meet and their contact information. Follow up with people after you meet them, and stay in touch even if you don't have anything specific to say. Just a quick "thinking of you" message can go a long way in maintaining relationships. Sometimes **the personal touch of a handwritten note or a phone call can make all the difference.** And, don't forget the importance of face-to-face communication. In today's world, it is easy to rely on text messages, emails, and social media, but nothing can replace good old-fashioned human interaction.

Finally, **don't be afraid to ask for what you want.** If there is someone you would like to meet or something you would like to achieve, reach out and ask for assistance. The worst that can happen is that they say no.

Building a strong network takes time and effort, but it is worth it. A strong network will provide you with support, advice, and opportunities when you need them.

How to Write a Professional Email

Emails can be pretty informal, which is great if you're contacting friends and family, but what about when you need to communicate with a potential employer or other professionals? In these cases, try to make sure that your email is clear, concise and free of any errors.

Here are a few tips for writing a professional email:

- **Use a clear and concise subject line.** This will help the recipient know what the email is about.

- **Keep it short and to the point.** No one wants to read long, rambling emails.

- **Use proper grammar and spelling.** This shows that you are taking the email seriously.

- **Appropriately address the recipient.** For example, if you're writing to David Kennedy, you would write "Dear Mr. Kennedy." If you don't know the person's name, it's OK to use "To whom it may concern" or "Dear sir/madam."

- **Avoid using abbreviations or slang.** Again, this is formal communication, so you want to use proper language.

- **Use a professional sign-off and signature.** For example, "Sincerely" or "Best wishes" as your sign-off, and for your signature, include your name, job title (if appropriate), and contact information.

By following these simple tips, you can ensure that your professional email makes the right impression.

How to Celebrate Family Members and Never Forget a Birthday

It can be tough to keep track of all the important dates in your life, let alone remember to celebrate them. However, when you leave home, it's important to show your loved ones how much you care, and one way to do that is by making sure you never forget a birthday.

Here are a few tips for celebrating family members and never forgetting a birthday:

- **Keep a calendar.** This will help you keep track of all the important dates in your life.

- **Set reminders.** Whether it's a reminder on your phone or a note in your planner, make sure you have some way to remind yourself of upcoming birthdays at least a week in advance.

- **Make a list.** Write down the birthdays of all your immediate family members and close friends in one place so you can refer to it when needed.

- **Get creative.** If you're struggling to develop gift ideas, think outside the box. The personal touch of a homemade card or gift can go a long way.

By following these simple tips, you can make sure you never forget another important date again.

Building Foundations for Healthy Relationships

As young adults, we are inundated with messages about what a "healthy" relationship looks like. Whether on social media, in magazines, or on TV, we are bombarded with images and stories about perfect relationships.

But what does a healthy relationship look like?

There is no one-size-fits-all answer to this question, as every relationship is different. However, we can all strive for some key characteristics of healthy relationships.

Some of the key characteristics of healthy relationships include:

- mutual respect,
- trust,
- communication,
- support, and
- equality.

In a healthy relationship, **both partners should feel valued and respected.** There should be **trust between you, and you should both feel comfortable communicating** openly with each other.

You should also feel supported by each other, and you should share equally in the relationship.

Of course, no relationship is perfect, and there will be times when things are not as smooth sailing as we would like them to be. But if you can work through these times together, and you still feel respected, valued, and equal in the relationship, then this is a good sign that you have a healthy relationship.

There are many different types of relationships, and no one type is better than another. What matters most is that you feel happy and safe in your relationship. If you are ever feeling unsafe or uncomfortable in a relationship, it's essential to reach out for help. Talk to a trusted friend or family member, or contact a service that offers support and advice.

No matter what type of relationship you are in, remember that **you deserve to be treated with respect and equality. We all have a right to a healthy and happy relationship.**

Chapter 8

HOW TO MANAGE A HOME

As you begin to live on your own, you'll quickly realize that there's much more to managing a home than just cleaning and cooking. There are also repairs, maintenance, and learning to use household appliances. It can be a lot to handle, but don't worry—we're here to help. In this chapter, we'll give you some tips on managing your home so you can keep everything running smoothly.

How to Use Household Appliances

How to Use an Oven

Using an oven is pretty simple—you just set the temperature and timer and wait for your food to cook. However, you should keep a few things in mind to ensure that your food turns out perfectly.

▸ **Preheat the oven.** This is especially important if you're baking, as it helps the food cook evenly.

▸ **Read the recipe and get the right temperature** for your oven. Every recipe is different, so make sure you know what temperature you need to set your oven.

▸ **Adjust your interchangeable oven racks,** depending on what the cooking instructions say. For example, if it says to cook the food on the top shelf, make sure you adjust your oven racks accordingly.

▸ **Know when to open the door.** Whenever you open the door, heat escapes, and it takes longer for the food to cook. So only open it when necessary.

▸ **Never leave food unattended.** This is a safety hazard, and it's also a surefire way to ruin your food.

By following these simple tips, you can ensure that your food turns out perfectly every time.

How to Use a Dishwasher

Dishwashers are a great way to get your dishes clean quickly and easily, but there are a few things you should keep in mind to ensure that they come out in good condition.

- **Read the manual.** The first thing you should do is read the manual for your dishwasher. This will tell you how to use it properly and maintain it.

- **Pre-wash your dishes.** You should always pre-wash your dishes before putting them in the dishwasher. This helps remove any food particles that could clog the machine or end up on your dishes.

- **Load the dishwasher properly.** It's important to load the dishwasher properly so that your dishes come out clean. There are usually specific racks for different types of dishes.

- **Use suitable detergent.** Make sure you use the correct type of detergent for your dishwasher. Some dishwashers have specific types of detergents that they need to work correctly.

- **Don't overload the machine** as it could stop the spinner that distributes the water and cleaning fluid effectively.

- **Select a wash cycle.** Insert the dishwasher tablet or cream into the tablet compartment usually located on the inner part of the door, and then start the dishwasher. Generally, the eco cycle is good enough to clean your pots but familiarize yourself with your machine and choose the most appropriate cycle.

- **Care for your machine.** Try to clean the dishwasher filter regularly. This helps prevent a build-up of food particles and keeps your device running smoothly. You should also add salt into the machine compartment every few months to help it run effectively.

By following these simple tips, you can ensure that your dishes come out clean every time.

How to do Your Laundry

Doing your laundry is often seen as a rite of passage for young adults. You might have relied on your parents or guardians to do this for you, but now it's time to learn how to do it yourself.

It's not always as simple as throwing your clothes in the washing machine and forgetting about them.

How to Use a Washing Machine

Using a washing machine is pretty straightforward—you just add your clothes, detergent, and water and set the machine to the proper cycle. However, you should keep a few things in mind to ensure that your clothes come out clean and in good condition.

- **Read the care labels.** The care labels on your clothes will tell you what cycle to use and the max temperature the water should be. If clothes are heavily soiled, they will need a hotter wash, whereas if the clothes are reasonably clean, you could use a low-temperature or quick wash. The faster the wash and lower the temperature, the less energy you're using.

How to Manage a Home

Wash	Do not wash	Hand wash only	Machine wash normal	Machine wash permanent press	Machine wash gentle	
	30 — Wash at or below 30 °C	40 — Wash at or below 40 °C	50 — Wash at or below 50 °C	60 — Wash at or below 60 °C	70 — Wash at or below 70 °C	95 — Wash at or below 95 °C
Iron	Do not iron	Do not steam	Iron any temp steam	Low temperature	Medium temperature	High temperature
Bleach	Do not bleach	Do not bleach	Bleach	Non-chlorine bleach		
Dry	Do not tumble dry	Tumble dry normal	Tumble dry permanent press	Tumble dry delicate gentle	Tumble dry low heat	Tumble dry medium heat	Tumble dry high heat	Tumble dry no heat
	Dry	Dry flat	Drip dry	Hang to dry	Do not wring	
Dry clean	Do not wet clean	A — Any solvent	F — Petroleum solvent only	P — Any solvent except tetrachloroethylene	W — Wet cleaning	Dry clean
	Do not dry clean	Reduced moisture	No steam	Low heat	Short cycle	

▸ **Separate your clothes.** You should always separate your clothes by color and fabric type. This helps to prevent them from bleeding or getting damaged in the wash.

▸ **Add the detergent.** Make sure you add the right amount of detergent—too much and your clothes will be stiff and rigid. Too little and they won't be as clean as you want them to be.

▸ **Don't overload the machine.** Try not to overload the washing machine, as this can damage your clothes and the machine itself. As a rough guide: A small load will be a third of the drum, and a medium load will be half of the drum. A full load is when the drum is packed three-quarters full.

- **Choose the correct cycle.** Different fabrics need different washing cycles, so make sure you use the correct one for your clothes. For example, if you're washing delicate items, you should use the delicate cycle.

- **Remove clothes after washing.** Once the washing cycle finishes, remove your clothes from the machine as soon as possible. Leaving them in there for too long can cause them to start growing mold or mildew making them smell.

Now you have clean clothes, let's look at the most effective ways to dry them.

How to Use a Tumble Dryer

Tumble dryers are a great way to get your clothes dry quickly, but there are a few things you should keep in mind.

- **Read the care labels.** The care labels on your clothes will tell you if they can be tumble-dried or not. If they can, it will also tell you what cycle to use. Not all clothes can be tumble dried, so check first, as this could make your clothes shrink, be damaged or misshapen.

- **Spin your clothes before you put them in the tumble dryer.** The more water removed from your clothes before they go in the tumble dryer, the quicker they will dry.

- **Use the right cycle.** Different fabrics need different drying cycles, so make sure you use the correct one for your clothes. For example, use the delicate cycle if you're drying delicate items.

- **Don't overload the machine.** As with the washing machine, do not overload the tumble dryer, as this can damage your clothes and the machine.

- **Look after your dryer.** Depending on your dryer, you may need to clean the filter after each use. This helps prevent a build-up of lint, which can be a fire hazard. You may also need to empty the water container that collects the water from your clothes.

Finally, you don't need to tumble dry all of your clothes. Some clothes, like jeans, can be hung up to dry. This will save you money on your electricity bill, but it will also help your clothes last longer.

How to Remove Stains

Removing stains is another part of doing your laundry. You need to treat stains as soon as possible; otherwise, they will set and be much harder to remove. There are many Stain Remover products on the market, but not everything works on every stain.

Here are a few stain removal tips:

- Use dish soap. Dish soap is great for removing grease stains. Just apply some to the stain and scrub it with a brush or sponge. Soak the item before washing as usual.
- Use toothpaste to remove grass stains. That's right. If you have a grass stain, just apply some toothpaste to the area and scrub. Rinse it off and then wash as normal.
- Make your stain remover for those hard to remove stains. Make a paste, using an equal part of white vinegar to an equal amount of baking soda, and apply it to the stain. Leave it for 10-15 minutes, and then add to a bucket of water with detergent and two tablespoons of vinegar. Soak overnight and then wash as usual.
- **Top TIP:** This Homemade stain remover is also effective on carpet stains. Use a toothbrush or scrubbing brush to scrub the paste mixture into the stain, and then wash it out with soap and water.

How to Clean Your Home

Keeping your home clean and tidy is an important skill. It is good for your health and wellbeing, and it will also make a good impression on guests.

Here are some simple tips that will help you keep your home clean:

- **Develop a cleaning routine and stick to it.** Having a set routine will help you keep on top of the cleaning and ensure you don't miss anything. If you live in a shared house, allocate specific tasks to each person every week. For example, one person could be responsible for hoovering, while another person is responsible for cleaning the kitchen.

- **Don't let the dirt and mess build up.** The more you leave it, the harder it will be to clean. Do a little bit every day, and it will soon become part of your routine. This is particularly true for washing up. It's quicker and easier to wash up after a meal than leaving it until the evening.

- **Invest in good quality cleaning products.** Cheap cleaning products may be tempting, but they are often ineffective and don't last as long. It is worth spending a little extra on products that will do a better job.

- **Make your cleaning products.** There are recipes for cleaning products that you can make yourself, using things like vinegar, lemon juice, and bicarbonate of soda. These are environmentally friendly, but they are also usually much cheaper than shop-bought products.

Cleaning your home doesn't have to be a chore. By following these simple tips, you can develop a quick and easy routine to follow.

How to make your surface cleaner:

Making your own surface cleaner is easy and cheaper than buying shop-bought cleaners. You can make a simple surface cleaner using white vinegar, water, half a lemon, and essential oils.

To make a surface spray, you will need:

- A spray bottle
- 1 cup of white wine vinegar
- 15 drops of essential oil (peppermint, orange, lemon or lavender will work well)
- The juice of half of a lemon
- 1 cup of water

Method:

Add the ingredients to the spray bottle and shake gently.

Use this cleaner to wipe down surfaces in your home. It is particularly effective at removing grease and grime.

How to make your window cleaner:

Window cleaners can be expensive, but you can easily make your own using vinegar and water.

Mix 1 part white vinegar with two parts water in a spray bottle. Spray onto windows and wipe clean with a cloth.

You can also add a few drops of essential oil to your window cleaner to give it a pleasant scent.

How to Change Your Bedding

You spend around eight hours a day in bed, and though you may not know it or see it, your bedding can harbor all sorts of bacteria. That's why you should change your sheets and pillowcases every 1-2 weeks.

Here's how to do it:

1. Remove all of the old bedding from the bed, including the sheets, duvet cover, and pillowcases.
2. Wash all of the bedding following the care instructions. Generally, bedding should go on a hotter wash to kill any bacteria.
3. Once the bedding is clean, put it back on the bed, starting with the bottom sheet.
4. Turn your duvet cover inside out and put each top corner on your quilt or duvet Then, turn the duvet cover the right way, over the quilt or duvet cover. You may need to keep a tight hold of the corners while doing this, and then once you have it in place, simply hold the corners and give the cover a firm shake.
5. Put your pillows back in their pillowcases and plump them up.

Your bed is now fresh and clean and ready for a good night's sleep! Finally, it's a good habit to make your bed each day. No matter how bad your day has been, coming home to a made bed can make all the difference.

How to Unclog a Sink

Sometimes, your sink may get clogged, which means it's unable to drain effectively. You can do some things to fix this yourself, which means you will not have to pay for a plumber.

- First, you should try to use **boiling water.**
- Pour around half a gallon of boiling water directly into the drain.
- Let it sit for a few minutes to see if this does the trick.
- If not, you can try using a plunger.

Place the plunger over the drain and make sure there is enough water in the sink to cover the rubber part of the plunger. Push and pull the plunger up and down vigorously for around 30 seconds. When you remove the plunger, see if the water drains quickly, and if not, repeat the process.

There are powerful chemical drain cleaners available if you still have issues, but you could also make your own with a mix of vinegar and baking soda. Simply remove any water from the drain and pour in one cup of baking soda, followed by one cup of white vinegar. Cover the drain and leave the mixture for 15 minutes. Next, remove the stop and run the hot tap or use the boiling water to break up the clog.

How to Unclog a Toilet

If your toilet is clogged, don't panic! There are a few things you can do to try and fix it yourself before having to call a plumber.

The most effective way to unclog a toilet is to **use a plunger.**

- Simply insert this into the toilet bowl and cover the hole at the bottom, so the plunger is fully submerged.
- Slowly, pump the plunger up and down over the hole, and then build up the speed until you pump vigorously.
- To check if the toilet is unblocked, simply flush.
- Repeat as necessary until the blockage is cleared.

There are many drain cleaners you can buy for your toilet too, but you can also make your own.

Make your own drain cleaner:

- Wear rubber gloves, then add 1 cup of baking soda and 2 cups of vinegar to the toilet. The mixture will fizz.
- Pour half a gallon of hot water into the pot—it's best to pour this from your waist level as the force can help unclog the blockage.
- Make sure the water isn't boiling as this can crack the toilet.
- Leave the mixture overnight if possible, and then flush the next day.

Basic Sewing

If an item of clothing needs stitching or fixing, it can be expensive. Sometimes it's best to try to mend it yourself. Hand sewing is fast and easy, so it's worth trying.

You will need a basic sewing kit of threads (in different colors, mainly black and white), scissors, and at least one sewing needle.

How to mend a hole in fabric:

You will need:

- Thread
- A needle
- A piece of fabric or patch (optional)

Method:

1. **Unravel your cotton thread from the spool** — you should choose the thread closest to the color of the fabric you are stitching. When you've unraveled enough, cut the thread from the spool.

2. If you're using a patch, **place it over the hole** so that the good side of the fabric is facing out.

3. **Thread your needle and knot the end.** To do this, thread the cotton through the eye of the needle. Tie the ends of the thread in a knot at the bottom a couple of times to ensure it's secure. Now you're ready to stitch.

4. **Start sewing at the edge of the hole,** making small stitches close together. To do this , push the needle up through the fabric from the back (wrong side). Push the needle down through the other side.

5. **Repeat steps 2 and 3** around the entire edge of the hole.

6. When you're happy that the patch or hole is secure, **sew back and forth in the same place a couple of times,** and then knot the thread on the back of the fabric and snip off the excess.

There you have it! You've now successfully mended a hole in fabric.

How to sew on a button:

You will need:

- Thread
- A needle
- A button

Method:

1. **Thread your needle and knot the end.**
2. **Push the needle up through the fabric from the back,** making sure to come up through one of the holes in the button.
3. **Push the needle down through the other hole in the button.**
4. **Repeat steps 2 and 3** a few times to secure the button.
5. When you're happy that the button is secure, **knot the thread on the back** of the fabric and snip off the excess.

There you have it! You've now successfully sewn a button onto an item of clothing.

Chapter 9

ORGANIZATION & TIME MANAGEMENT

Being organized can save you time, money, and a lot of stress. It can also make your space look neater and more inviting on a practical level. When we are disorganized, it can lead to lost items, late fees, and a general feeling of being overwhelmed. **Developing good organization skills** managing your time effectively, and prioritizing your tasks are key to leading a productive and stress-free life.

Start with a Clean Bedroom

When you first leave home, your bedroom may double as your living room, home office, and dining room. Try to keep it clean and organized to be a sanctuary for you—a place where you can relax and unwind after a long day.

1. **Create designated spaces.** If your bedroom is a dumping ground for all of your stuff, it's time to change that. Create designated areas for different items — a place for your clothes, a place for your school things, your books, etc. This will help you to keep things organized and tidy.
2. **Create a workspace.** If you don't have a designated workspace in your bedroom, it's time to create one. It could be a desk or table, but this will be where you can do your homework, work on projects, etc. Try to avoid using it for other tasks, such as eating or watching tv. Your workspace should be uncluttered and clear of any distractions to help you stay focused and organized.
3. **Get rid of the clutter.** Take a good look around your room and get rid of anything you don't need or use. This will help clear up some space and make it easier to keep things tidy.
4. **Invest in some storage solutions.** If you don't have enough closet space, consider buying a dresser or some shelving to store your things. This will help you to keep your items organized and off of the floor.
5. **Make your bed every day.** Taking a few minutes each day to make your bed will go a long way in making your room look neat.
6. **Do a "10-minute tidy" every night before going to bed.** This means taking 10 minutes to pick up any clutter accumulated during the day.
7. **Prepare for tomorrow today.** Get your clothes and school supplies ready for the next day before going to bed. This will help you avoid scrambling in the morning and make it easier to get out the door on time.

How to Create a Productive Workspace

Creating a productive workspace is essential if you want to be able to focus on your studies and get work done. It doesn't have to be extensive or elaborate—**just a simple, uncluttered space where you can sit down and concentrate on your task.** You may have a dedicated room that you can use as your workspace, or you may have to create a space in your bedroom. Either way, you can do a few things to make sure it's conducive to productivity.

Firstly, it's a good idea to **pick somewhere solely for work**—a place where you can sit down and focus without any distractions. You should **avoid using your bed or sofa** as a workspace, as it's too easy to get comfortable and fall asleep! If you don't have a dedicated room for your workspace, try to create a space that is separate from the rest of your bedroom so that you can mentally 'switch off' when you're finished working for the day and 'switch on' when it's time to study.

It's also important to **make sure your workspace is well-lit.** Natural light is always best, so try to position your desk near a window. If you don't have access to natural light, make sure you have a good-quality lamp to light up your work area.

Make sure your workspace is comfortable. This means having a comfy chair and a suitable desk or table at the correct height. The likelihood is you will be at your desk for long periods, so **make sure you're comfortable to avoid any strain on your back or neck.** Your computer should be at eye level, and your arms should be at a 90-degree angle when you're typing. You may find that a standing desk is more comfortable, or that you prefer to work in short bursts with regular breaks—there is no 'correct' way to do it, so find what works best for you.

Finally, your workspace should also be **uncluttered and organized.** This means having a place for everything and keeping your desk tidy. A messy desk can distract you and make it harder for you to focus on your work. Invest in some storage solutions, such as baskets or boxes, to help you keep things tidy. And try to avoid working from your bed, as this can make it harder to focus and be productive.

Organizing and Storing Documents

As you get older, you'll acquire a lot of paperwork and documents, such as school records, medical records, tax documents, bills, etc. Try to keep these organized so that you can easily find them when you need them. The best way to do this is to **create a filing system.**

You can **either buy** a pre-made filing system **or create your own** using labels and folders. Start by creating a main folder for each document category (e.g., school, medical, tax, etc.) Then, create sub-folders for each document within that category. For example, you might have a 'school' folder with sub-folders by subject or topic.

Label your folders clearly to easily find what you're looking for. Date each document and file, so your most recent documents are at the top. And try to keep on top of it by **regularly sorting files** and purging outdated or unnecessary documents.

Filing digital documents is much the same as filing physical documents. Start by creating folders for each document category, then sub-folders for each document within that category. **Date your documents to easily find what you're looking for.** For example, you might have a folder on your computer called 'Medical Records' with sub-folders for ' immunization records,' 'doctor visits,' and 'prescriptions.' A document within 'immunization records' might be labeled 'MMR immunization — date.'

You can also use online storage services, such as Google Drive or Dropbox to store and organize your documents. These services allow you to access your files from any device with an internet connection, which can be handy if you need to retrieve a copy while you're on the go. Remember to **back up your files regularly** in case of a technical malfunction or power outage.

Backing up Files

No matter how organized and well-maintained your computer is, things can always go wrong. Hard drives can crash, power outages can happen, and accidental deletions are not uncommon. That's why **it's important to back up your files regularly.**

Backing up your files means making copies of them and storing them in a safe place, such as an external hard drive or a cloud-based storage service. If something happens to your computer, you can rest assured knowing that you have a backup of all your files.

There are a few different ways to go about backing up your files. **You can do it manually,** which means making copies of your files and storing them in a safe place regularly. **Or you can use automatic backup software,** which will make copies of your files and keep them in a safe place without you having to do anything. Some operating systems, such as Windows and macOS, even come with their own built-in backup software.

No matter which method you choose, the important thing is to ensure that your backup files are stored safely, such as an external hard drive or a cloud-based storage service. And remember to check that your backup files are up-to-date regularly.

Time Management

One of the most essential life skills that every young adult should learn is time management. Time management is all about **using your time wisely** to get the most out of each day. **It's a skill** that can be learned and practiced, and it will come in handy both in college and in the working world.

Managing Study and Work

When studying or working, it's vital to manage your time wisely. To manage this effectively, you should make full use of your diary. **Use your diary to mark down deadlines, upcoming events, and other important dates.** This will help you stay on top of things and ensure that you don't miss anything important.

You should also **break down big tasks into smaller,** more manageable chunks. For example, if you have a project due in two weeks, break the project down into smaller tasks that you can complete each day. This will make the project seem less daunting and **help you prioritize** your time effectively.

Make a plan and stick to it, and while it's easy to take things on, **be careful that you don't take on too much.** Many people find the 'working backward' technique helpful for managing their time. This involves starting with the end goal in mind and working backward to figure out what steps you need to take to achieve it. For example, if your goal is to finish a project by the end of the week, **start by figuring out what tasks need to be completed each day** to reach that goal.

Finally, **schedule some free time into your day.** This may seem like a waste of time, but it's crucial for your mental and physical health. Make sure to schedule some time each day to relax and do something you enjoy. This could be anything from reading a book to going for a walk. The important thing is that you take some time to unwind and recharge each day.

How to Prioritize Effectively

It can be difficult to prioritize, as you are ultimately deciding between one task and another. However, some general tips can **help you** when it comes to prioritizing.

Make a list of all your tasks. Identify which are urgent and time-sensitive. Then identify the important tasks that are not necessarily urgent but still important to do. Once you have identified the urgent and important tasks, you can start to prioritize them.

Some people find it helpful to use a **priority matrix** when figuring out which tasks to prioritize. This is a visual way of representing the urgency and importance of each job. Place the tasks into one of four quadrants based on their urgency and importance.

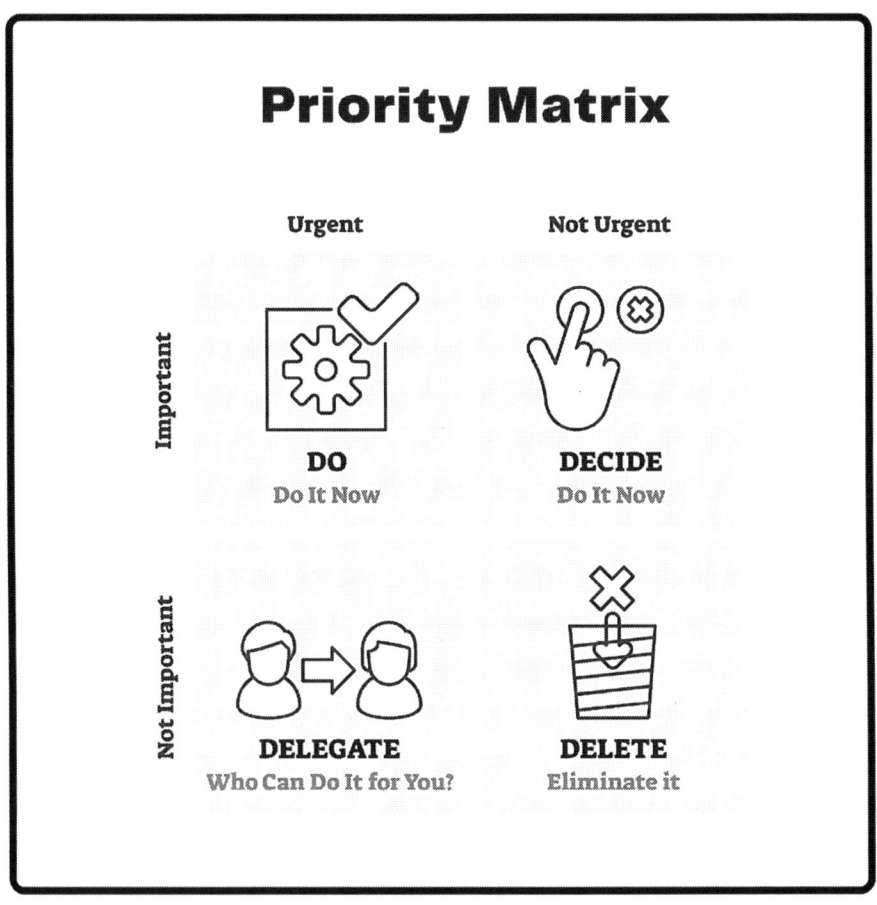

- **The first quadrant is for tasks that are both urgent and important.** These are the tasks that you should prioritize first.

- **The second quadrant is for tasks that are important but not urgent.** You should schedule these tasks into your diary or to-do list.

- **The third quadrant is for tasks that are urgent but not important.** These are the tasks that you should delegate to someone else.

- **The fourth quadrant is for tasks that are neither urgent nor important.** These are the tasks that you can eliminate from your to-do list altogether.

Once you have prioritized your tasks, it's important to stick to your plan. Don't let other tasks that come up distract you from the task at hand. It can be challenging to stay focused, but if you can maintain your focus, you will be able to accomplish your goals more efficiently.

Goal Setting

When setting goals, you should always think first about the result. What is it you want to achieve? What are you aiming for? When do you want to hit your goal? It's helpful to be invested in the goal, so ensure it's something you want—if it's not, it's unlikely you will be willing to put the time and effort into achieving it.

Once you have a goal in mind, you need to ensure it's SMART. This means it must be Specific, Measurable, Attainable, Relevant, and Time-bound.

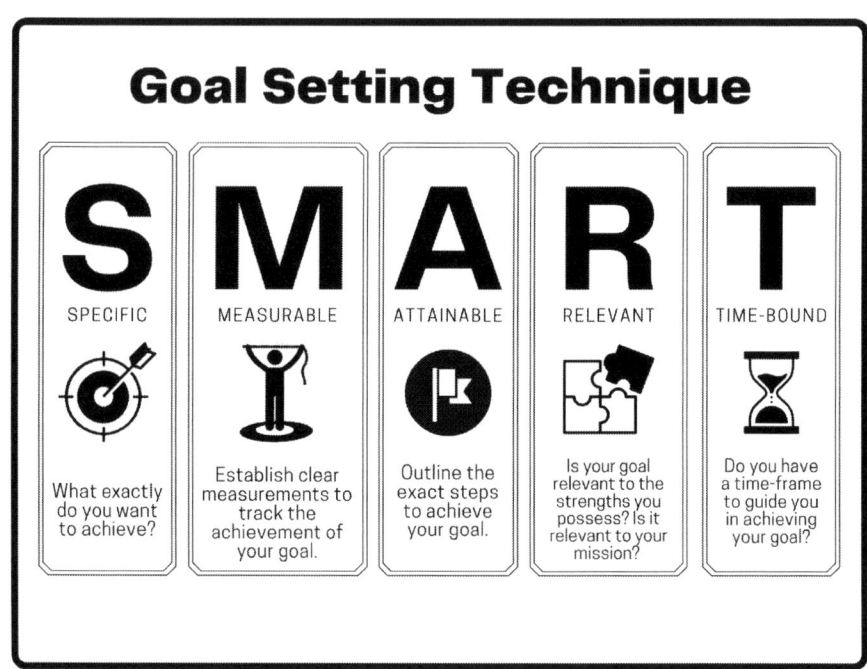

For example, if your goal is to complete a history assignment that is due in four weeks, your stated initial goal might be:

'I will complete my history assignment by reading one chapter of my textbook each day'

In the above example, the goal is specific (reading one chapter of the textbook), measurable (I will mark each day off in my calendar as I complete it), attainable (I can realistically read one chapter per day), realistic (I have four weeks to complete the assignment) and time-bound (my assignment is due in four weeks)

Now it's time to break your goals down. You can do this by asking yourself several questions as you start at your end goal and work backward.

For example, if your goal is to complete an assignment in four weeks, you might ask yourself the following:

- How many pages do I need to read each day?
- What steps must be completed before I start reading?
- When will I complete my research and outline?

By answering these questions, you'll have a better understanding of what needs to be done in order to complete your goal.

By breaking your goals down into smaller, more achievable steps and ensuring that they are SMART, you can set yourself up for success and effectively manage your time. With the right approach, anyone can learn to effectively manage their time and make the most of each day.

Chapter 10

SOLVING PROBLEMS & DECISION-MAKING SKILLS

Every day we face a multitude of decisions, big and small. Some of these decisions are easy to make, while others may be more difficult. The same goes for problem-solving. Some problems are easy to solve, while others may be more challenging.

Problem-solving and decision-making are closely linked. Problems often present us with a dilemma, and we must use our decision-making skills to choose the best course of action.

In this chapter, we're going to take a look at some of the skills you need to make decisions and solve problems effectively.

Life Skills for Young Adults

Problem Solving Skills

Problems are a part of everyday life, and rather than ignoring them; it's best to tackle them head-on before they escalate. They can be small, like trying to figure out what to wear to your friend's party, or big, like deciding which college to attend.

No matter the size of the problem, there is a process that you can follow to help you solve it. This process is known as the **'problem-solving cycle.'** This is a skill you can carry with you in everything you do. It will help you in your career, personal life, and studies.

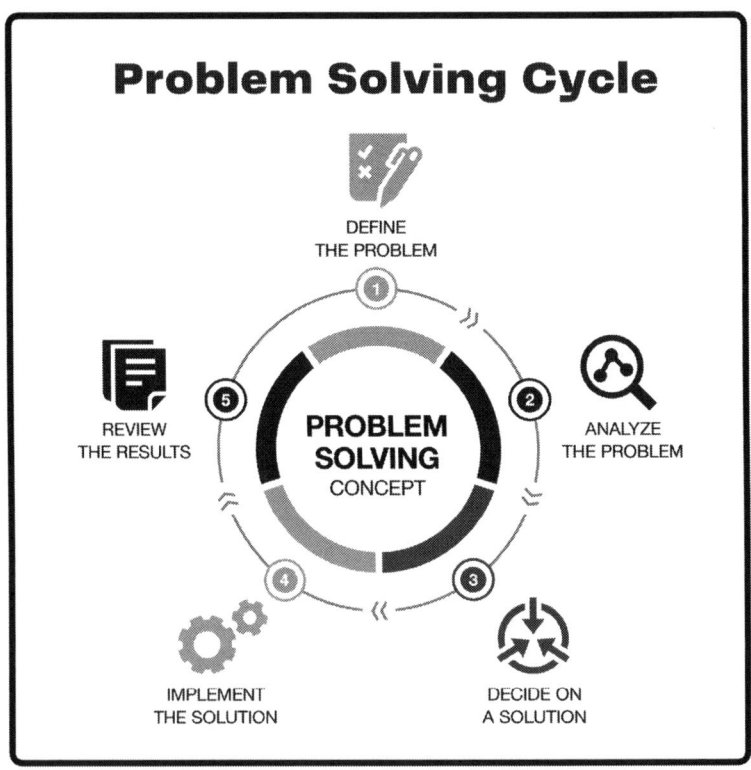

- **The first step in the problem-solving cycle is to define the problem.** This may seem like an obvious first step, but take the time to determine what the problem is. Once you have identified the problem, you can start to brainstorm possible solutions.

- **The second step is to analyse the problem and evaluate the possible solutions.** Once you have generated a list of possible solutions, it's time to evaluate them. Consider the pros and cons of each solution. What are the risks and potential benefits of each solution?

- **The third step is to choose the best solution.** After evaluating the possible solutions, it's time to choose the one you think is best.

- **The fourth step is to implement the solution.** Once you have chosen the best solution, it's time to put it into action. This may involve steps such as buying the supplies you need or telling your friends and family about your decision.

- **The final step is to review the results.** How did you do? What would you do differently next time? Making mistakes is all part of the process; try to look back objectively at what you have done and how you might change things next time around.

It's important to remember that not all problems can be solved. And sometimes, the best solution is to do nothing at all.

Decision Making

We make decisions every day, big and small. Some of these decisions are easy to make and require little or no thought, like what to eat for breakfast. Other choices may be more complex, and need us to weigh up the pros and cons of each option.

Making big decisions can feel like a huge responsibility. You may feel anxious, stressed and even unsure of yourself. But remember, decisions are empowering. They allow you to take control of your life and create the future you want.

There is no 'right' or 'wrong' way to decide. But there are some steps that you can follow to help you make the best decision for you.

▶ Firstly, when you faced with difficult decisions, it can be helpful to **take some time to think about what you want.** What are your goals and values? What is important to you? Once you have a good understanding of what you want, you can consider your options.

▶ The next step is to **gather information about your options.** This may involve doing some research or talking to people who have expertise. Consider the 'What Ifs.' What if you make this decision? What are the risks and potential benefits? What if you don't make this decision? You might find it helpful to write a list of the pros and cons of each option. By writing down our thoughts and feelings, we can often start to see the situation more clearly.

▶ The third step is to **make a decision.** Once you have gathered all the information you need, it's time to decide. Trust your gut and go with your instincts. But also be prepared to change your mind if new information comes to light.

- And finally, once you have made your decision, it's time to **take action.** This may involve steps such as buying the supplies you need or telling your friends and family about your decision.

Remember, making decisions is empowering. It allows you to take control of your life and create the future you want. So next time you're faced with a difficult decision, don't be afraid to trust your gut and go for it!

Better Decision Making

Better decision-making comes from experience. The more you practice making decisions, the better you will become at it. Equally, knowing yourself and what is important will also help you make better decisions.

- Firstly, **consider your characteristics and personality type.** Are you an impulsive, or do you like to take your time? Do you want to take risks or play it safe? Knowing your personal preferences can help you understand how you might approach making decisions.

- Secondly, **think about the situation you are in and what is important to you** at that moment. What are your goals and values? What do you want to achieve? Understanding what is important to you will help you make better decisions.

- Thirdly, **slow down and take your time:** When faced with a difficult decision, it can be tempting to just go with your first instinct. But slow down and take the time to think about your options. Don't be pressured or rushed into making a decision.

- Finally, **don't be afraid to make mistakes**—we all do! Just learn from them and keep going.

Making decisions is a normal part of life. The more you practice, the better you will become at it. And by understanding yourself and what is important to you, you can make better decisions for yourself.

How to Say NO!

In our fast-paced, constantly connected world, it's easy to overcommit and take on more than we can handle. So learning to say no, is a crucial skill every young person should learn.

Saying no can be difficult, especially if we don't want to disappoint other people. But it's important to remember that we can't do everything and that it's okay to say no.

Saying no can be difficult, especially if we don't want to disappoint other people. But it's important to remember that we can't do everything and that **it's okay to say no.** If there's something you don't want to do or something that you cannot do, then the best thing to do is, to be honest and just say no. Don't prolong the situation, just say the word.

Solving Problems & Decision-Making Skills

> **Here are some tips for how to say no:**
>
> ▶ **Be polite but firm in your decision.** "I'm sorry, but I can't help you with that." Showing people that when you make a decision will help them respect your choices. While they may be disappointed, they will understand that you have made up your mind.
>
> ▶ **Be honest and explain your reasons for saying no.** "I'm sorry, but I'm just not comfortable doing that." This can help the other person understand where you are coming from and why you have made this decision.
>
> ▶ **Offer an alternative solution.** "I can't do that, but maybe I can do this instead." If there is another way that you can help, let the person know. This shows that you are still willing to help, but in a way that works better for you.

Saying no is not always easy, but it is an important life skill to learn. It can help you manage your time and commitments, and it can also help you set boundaries with other people. You may find yourself in situations where you feel under pressure to say yes. But it's important to remember that you have a right to say no. Even with friends and family, **you don't owe anyone anything.** It's OK to say no.

By being polite, honest, and offering alternatives, you can say no in a respectful and helpful way. Like all life skills, it takes practice, but with time and patience, you will get better at it with time and patience.

Chapter 11

KICKSTARTING YOUR CAREER

So, you've finished school or college, and you're ready to take on the world. Congratulations! **The next step is to find a job that you love.** But with the job market being so competitive, it can be hard to know where to start.

The one thing to remember is that if you persevere, you will get your opportunity, so don't give up!

>
> **Perseverance is failing 19 times and succeeding the 20th.**
>
> JULIE ANDREWS,
> ACTRESS

Job Hunting Tips

Before you start job hunting, take some time to **figure out what you want to do.** What are your skills and interests? What type of work environment do you want to be in? Once you understand what you want, you can start looking for jobs that match your criteria.

There are many different ways to look for jobs. You can search online job boards, browse company websites, or go old-school and look through the classifieds section in your local newspaper or the windows of retail or hospitality establishments that state they are hiring.

Another great way to find jobs is by **networking**. Talk to your friends, family, and acquaintances and let them know that you are looking for work. They may know of someone who is hiring, or they may be able to put in a good word for you.

It's also a good idea to **attend job fairs and industry events.** This is a great way to meet potential employers and learn about different companies that are recruiting.

Another possibility, if you have a skill or an idea, is to become an entrepreneur by starting your own business. This can be a great option if you are creative and motivated.

Once you have found a few potential jobs you are interested in, the next step is to apply for them.

Applying for a Job

When you apply for a job, you will usually need to submit a resume and a cover letter. This is your chance to sell yourself to the employer and explain why you are the best person for the job.

CV or Resume

A resume is a document that outlines your skills, experience, and qualifications. It is important to tailor your resume to each job that you apply for, as this will show the employer that you have the relevant skills and experience for the role.

Your resume should be clear and concise, and it should highlight your skills, qualifications, and experience. If you have little or no work experience, don't worry, you can include any relevant volunteer work, internships, or extracurricular activities that you have participated in.

How to Write a Resume that Converts

When writing a resume, make sure to:

▶ Summarise your key skills, qualities, and job titles. For example, if you worked in a café, you could introduce yourself as:
A highly skilled, motivated and reliable food service assistant, with excellent customer service skills and cash handling experience.

- Start with your **most recent job or experience and work backward.** Ensuring you include key details such as your job title, dates of employment, duties, and responsibilities.

- **Highlight your skills, qualities, and accomplishments,** ensuring you use keywords relevant to the job you are applying for. For example, if you are applying for a job as a barista, make sure to mention your experience making coffee and using different coffee machines.

- **Include transferable or soft skills** that may be relevant to the job you are applying for. For example, if you are applying for a customer service role, highlight your excellent communication and interpersonal skills.

- **Use simple language and action words** such as 'achieved,' 'created,' 'managed', or 'developed.'

- **Use clear formatting and include bullet points** rather than paragraphs so that it is easy to read.

- **Check your grammar and spelling.** Remember, the person reading your resume is likely to spend less than 30 seconds looking at it before they decide to put it down or keep reading.

- Make it interesting and memorable, but you should **NEVER lie on your CV/resume,** or any other job application you make, as you may be found out. Employers carry out checks on identity, references, qualifications and previous jobs or experience. It's not worth it—just be yourself; it's enough!

Your Cover Letter

A cover letter is a document that accompanies your resume when you apply for a job. It is an opportunity to introduce yourself to the employer and explain why you are interested in the role and why you would be the best person. Your cover letter should follow a simple format and **should be 1 page** in length.

Remember, this is a letter, so you should include your address and contact number on the right-hand side at the top, and the addressee's information on the left, just below yours.

Address the person you are writing to by name or 'Dear sir/madam,' Just below this greeting, you should introduce yourself and the role you are applying for. 'Please find my application enclosed for the position of X.'

The body of the letter should **outline your relevant skills and experience,** highlighting how they make you the ideal candidate for the job. For example, if you are applying for an office role, you could mention your experience working in a fast-paced environment and your ability to juggle multiple tasks simultaneously.

Use specific examples to back up your claims. For example, if you are claiming to be an excellent communicator, you could mention when you had to diffuse a difficult customer service situation.

Once you have outlined your relevant skills and experience, **finish with a strong conclusion,** thanking the employer for their time and expressing your interest in meeting with them to discuss the role further.

If you are mailing your application, **print your resume and cover letter on high-quality paper** and send them to the person or organization directly. If you are emailing your application, include your resume and cover letter as attachments and address the email to the relevant contact person. In the email body, explain who you are and why you are interested in the role.

Interview Tips for Beginners

Congratulations, you've got to the next stage. The company liked your resume and cover letter and has asked you to come in for an interview. Here are some tips on making a great impression and ace the interview.

Preparing for Your Interview

Failing to prepare is preparing to fail.

BENJAMIN GRAHAM,
ECONOMIST, PROFESSOR & INVESTOR

Before the interview, there are some things you can do to ensure you are prepared.

- **First, research the company.** Have a look at their website and social media platforms to get an idea of their culture, values, and what they do. If you can talk intelligently about the company, you are more likely to make a good impression and stand out from the crowd.

- **Second, research the role you are applying for.** This will help you understand what the company is looking for in a candidate and give you a better idea of how to sell yourself for the role.

- **Third, practice your answers to common interview questions.** This will help you feel more confident on the day and give you a better chance of impressing the interviewer.

> **Some common interview questions are:**
> - What are your strengths?
> - What are your weaknesses?
> - Why are you interested in this role?
> - What experience do you have in this field?
> - Where do you see yourself in five years?
> - How do you think you'd fit in with the core values and company mission?

Practice your interview answers with someone you know and ask them for feedback. Try to be as specific as possible and use examples to back up your claims. For instance, if you are claiming to be an excellent communicator, you could mention when you had to diffuse a difficult customer service situation.

- **Finally, prepare some questions to ask at the end of the interview.** Think about what you would like to know about the job or the company. You could ask about development or promotional opportunities or ask questions about the company values and mission. This again shows that you are interested in the role and company and helps you stand out from other candidates.

How to Nail Your Interview

It's interview day! Here are some final tips to help you make a great impression and ace the interview.

- **First, dress for success.** Make sure you have dressed appropriately for the role you are applying for. How formal is up to you, but it's always better to be overdressed than underdressed.

- **Second, arrive 10 to 15 minutes early.** This will allow you to collect your thoughts and relax before the interview starts. Take a drink of water with you and make a note of the person's name you're meeting so you can ask for them and greet them personally.

- **Third, turn off your phone and leave it in your bag.** You don't want to be distracted by notifications during the interview.

- **Fourth, be confident, positive, and try to relax.** Greet the interviewer confidently, make eye contact, and remember to smile during the interview. You have nothing to fear. Maintain a positive attitude throughout, demonstrating a whatever it takes attitude. When giving examples, always show your commitment!

▸ **Finally, listen carefully, answer the questions honestly and be yourself.** Keep your answers brief, and use the preparation you did beforehand to guide you. The interviewer is looking for a genuine person they can trust, so be honest and sincere and let your personality shine through.

After the interview, it's a good idea to **send a thank-you note to the interviewer.** This shows that you are interested in the role and company and helps you to stand out from other candidates.

How to Get Promoted FAST!

Congratulations, you got the job! Now the fun starts—it's time to start thinking about how to get promoted.

Getting promoted fast is all about getting noticed by your superiors and proving you are an asset to the company.

Here are some tips to help you get promoted fast:

1. **Learn your job quickly and do it well.** This sounds obvious, but focus on doing your best work every day. This will help you stand out from other employees and shows your dedication to the job.

2. **Learn about the organization and the industry.** This will help you understand how the company works and what is important to them. It will also give you a better idea of how you can contribute to the company's success.

3. **Be proactive,** and take on additional responsibilities. This will show that you are willing to go above and beyond your job description and that you can handle more responsibility. Take on new projects that challenge you and embrace changes — be a leader at learning new things and paving the way.

4. **Develop a 'can-do' attitude.** Don't be put off if something looks tricky, **do it anyway,** and if there's a problem, let your problem-solving skills shine!

5. **Ask Your Boss for Clear Expectations.** Keep performing to the best of your ability and make your career ambitions known to your boss. Make the best of your supervisions and performance reviews by gaining feedback from your boss and expressing your wishes for new opportunities (such as training or work shadowing).

6. **Show you're a leader** by acting as a leader and being heard! While it's important to be a team player, show you're a leader. Dress like a leader and lead whenever possible. When it comes to meeting targets and deadlines, rise to the occasion and encourage others in your team. At team meetings, always engage and contribute. Be innovative by trying new things, discussing new ideas, and encouraging others within your team to do the same.

7. **Make your growth opportunities,** don't wait for others. You could take on new tasks or embrace online training in specific topics that will compliment your current role. For example, if you're interested in becoming a team leader, look for learning opportunities in team leading.

8. Always **take the initiative** and make it easy. Don't make things difficult. Take tricky situations and simplify them, then teach others how to do it. For example, sometimes processes within a workplace are made more complicated than they should be, so if you know a better way, share it, model it, and teach it.

9. Don't be afraid to **ask for a promotion.** If you've been working hard and there's no chance of any opportunities, then look for employment elsewhere.

While these tips don't guarantee a promotion, you can increase your chances of being noticed and achieving success in your career by building the right attitude and mindset.

So, what are you waiting for? Get started today and start working towards your next promotion!

Self-Improvement and Education

Self-improvement is a journey, not a destination. You should constantly be striving for, regardless of where you are in life. Whether you're just starting in your career or you're a seasoned professional, there is always room for improvement.

Self-Improvement

Self-improvement takes many forms. It could be learning new skills, increasing your knowledge, or developing new attitudes and mindsets. Whatever form it takes, self-improvement is essential for furthering your career and achieving success.

One of the best ways to **improve yourself is through education.** You can make yourself more valuable to your organization and position yourself for future success by increasing your knowledge. There are many ways to educate yourself, including taking courses, attending seminars, and reading books and articles.

Educating yourself is all about adding to your toolbox of skills and knowledge to be more effective in your job, career, and personal life. It's about taking the time to invest in yourself to reap the rewards down the road.

By educating yourself, you get to decide the direction of your life. You get to control your destiny. Set yourself some goals, surround yourself with people who will support your dreams, and never stop learning. Your career and personal life will thank you for it!

Kickstarting Your Career

The best teacher in life is experience.

LEBRON JAMES,
BASKETBALL PLAYER

And finally, while you can educate yourself in many ways, one way you can't is by taking life experience. This is something that comes with age and maturity. The best way to gain life experience is simply by living life and making mistakes. It's all part of the journey!

So don't wait. Start your journey today! Good luck!

THANKS FOR READING MY BOOK!

I sincerely hope you enjoyed this book, and that you will benefit from implementing the Life Skills discussed.

I would be incredibly grateful if you could take a few seconds to leave me an honest review or a star-rating on Amazon. (A star-rating only takes a couple of clicks).

Your review helps other young adults discover this book, and may also help them on their life journey. It will also be good Karma for you.

IF YOU WOULD LIKE TO LEAVE A REVIEW

SCAN THE QR CODE BELOW TO GO DIRECTLY TO THE REVIEW PAGE.

SOMETHING FOR YOU!

Get your FREE Life Skills Printable Templates

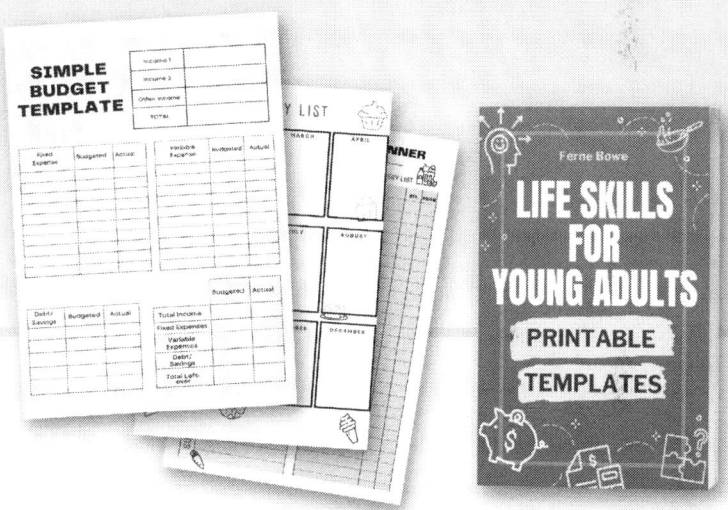

SCAN QR CODE TO GET YOUR COPY

Made in the USA
Columbia, SC
07 December 2022

9a201f43-f32a-483e-9de0-4023849d2ca1R01